Extreme Customer Service...
How to Give It!
How to Get It!

by Philip R. Nulman

Franklin Lakes, NJ

Just Say Yes!

Cover design by Foster & Foster

Printed in the U.S.A. by Book-mart Press

To order this title, please call toll-free 1-800-CAREER-1 (NJ and Canada: 201-848-0310) to order using VISA or MasterCard, or for further information on books from Career Press.

The Career Press, Inc., 3 Tice Road, PO Box 687, Franklin Lakes, NJ 07417

Library of Congress Cataloging-in-Publication Data

Nulman, Philip R., 1951-

Just say yes! : extreme customer service—How to give it! How to get it! / by Philip R. Nulman.

p. cm.

Includes index.

ISBN 1-56414-420-8 (pbk.)

1. Customer services. I. Title.

HF5415.5.N85 1999

658.8'12—dc21 99-046846

Table of Contents

Introduction
Just Say Yes! 7

Chapter 1
No Problem, No Problem, No Problem 9

Chapter 2
Unhappy Customers Don't Always Yell Back...
They Just Stop Coming 31

Chapter 3
Reach Them Where They Live:
The Magic of the Database 49

Chapter 4
Welcome to the Land of Big 59

Chapter 5
Civility and Common Sense 71

Chapter 6
Customer Service Starts With Common Sense 93

Chapter 7
Service Shmervice...All I Care About Is Price! 111

Chapter 8
Who Are These Customers...and Why Do They Say
Such Awful Things? 123

Chapter 9
Ask a Futurist Where Customers Are Headed! 135

Chapter 10
Mind Your Own Business 151

Chapter 11
Be Outrageous...As Long As You Create
the Right Rage 169

Chapter 12
Civility and Business...Mutually Exclusive? 181

Index 187

Dedication

To my father, Samuel Nulman, the most civilized man I ever met (1915–1971). There is a void in the world that will never be filled!

Introduction

Just Say Yes!

When I set out to write this book, my original intention was to include many personal frustrations to point out the enormous lack of service in this country. I believed that I would illustrate what should be done in business today. Indeed, I have a great number of examples of businesses treating people with hostility or blind indifference.

Something happened, though, as I researched the topic in preparation for writing *Just Say Yes*. It occurred to me that my job was to provide solutions, not problems. The book is based upon common sense coupled with principles that have worked. But, the bottom line is that behind every truly great company is a truly great credo regarding the customer. Sometimes we forget why we're in business.

Today, technology removes us farther from our customers, and as consumers, we feel the distance between the seller and ourselves as buyers. Technology will indeed change the face of business from this point forward...and in the process eliminate present means of distribution if we're not careful to stay closely connected to our customers. **Extreme customer service** is a system of romancing our customers in ways that cannot be duplicated through technology. And, while the Internet is evolving...industries that are truly dedicated to the principles of civility, humanity, creative compassion for the plight of the customer...will succeed in spite of high-tech options available to consumers.

Just Say Yes is about being polite and recognizing that our true task is not to sell products or services...but to sell the customer what they truly want and need. Everytime you encounter a customer, think in terms of building a relationship that can enhance your life from the point of civility and profitability. That's how many of the companies I've noted in the text began.

Remember too that the best form of communication you have in growing your business and achieving your goals is the customer. He or she is your advocate, your sales staff, your public relations firm and your future. Invest in the customer and the rest will fall into place. Just say yes!

Chapter 1

No Problem, No Problem, No Problem

You wake up in the morning (and, if you're like me) you shower, dress, pat the kids on the head, and leap into the driver's seat for the trek to work. Each morning the same ritual occurs. Usually, your expectations are low when it comes to receiving some amazing experience on your way to work.

Usually, my first encounter with another person is at the toll booth, where customer service is not only nonexistent, but not expected by anyone...except for me. "May I have a receipt please," I ask the toll collector politely. Now, I realize that toll collectors may not have the most glamorous job in the world and the fumes are a bit much, however, they've only got one task. You'd think that in order to make their jobs even a little bit more interesting, they'd acknowledge the customer who's dropping money in their hands for the privilege of driving on the road.

Customers? Are we *really* customers to the toll collector? The answer is a resounding yes. We are all both buyers and sellers, every day of our lives. The business they serve is the municipality or the state, but we're the customer using their service or product (however you wish to define the road system). Can we expect good service? Once again, the answer is yes. We should not only expect it but *demand* it. Even when a business has a complete monopoly on a particular product or service—

we can demand to be treated well. After all, what are we really demanding? We're demanding to be treated with respect and care as someone who supports that service or purchases that product. Once we recognize that, then the "just say yes" philosophy begins to make some sense.

Nordstrom is probably one of the most highly recognized service-driven companies in the United States today (and perhaps the world). Why is this? They've boiled down their reason for being in business into two words that they live by each and every day: *no problem*! "No problem" scrolls on the computer screens at their checkout terminals. No problem is their answer to their main question "What do you say to a customer in response to *any* request?"

If we buy into the "no problem" philosophy of business, then we really and truly empower the customer to be honest and to treat us with integrity. Will that happen all the time? No! But that's not a reason not to employ a service driven strategy of doing business. We have to recognize that the "no problem" philosophy has some slight risk...but statistically the risk is minimal and the rewards far greater.

The overwhelming majority of customers will simply not express dissatisfaction with a business. In fact, the percentage has been touted as 66 percent of those surveyed. If that's true then you will lose customers at an alarming rate by not listening to them. If you're the customer, you owe it to yourself and the business you're doing business with to communicate your needs as the customer. Customer service cannot exist without customer communication.

As consumers, we have indicated that we are unhappy with most of the businesses in our lives. I know that because I've read the reports and interviewed consumers and researched customers in every walk of life. If we examine the businesses we run into on a daily basis, we begin to recognize that for the most part, cynicism, skepticism, and even suspicion are prevalent in the business culture today. Business owners are convinced the customer is out to get them and customers are convinced that businesses are mercenary and uncaring. In truth, both can be right!

When the American Society for Quality Service conducted their survey, it wasn't poor service that scored high on the list of reasons why people abandon business relationships. It wasn't abuse that scored high—it was indifference. Of those surveyed, 68 percent indicated that they would leave a business relationship as a customer if treated with indifference by an employee. Why? Emotionally, we have nowhere to go with an indifferent person. If they treat us poorly, we can react, fight back, register an official complaint—even take legal action. But when we encounter someone who treats us with indifference, there's nowhere to go. What do we say? "The waiter stared into space when we were ordering and he didn't seem interested in us?" It doesn't work.

What does it really take to make us happy?

Believe it or not, it takes very little to make customers happy. Customer service relates directly to emotions. So, when we encounter a warm smile or a confident salesperson who appears amiable and knowledgeable, we're putty in their hands. Psychologists refer to this as "conditioned response." We respond to the nature of the stimulus as it's presented to us. We can manipulate customers as business owners and can be manipulated as customers by business simply by our body language, nonverbal communication, words, touch, demeanor, etc. It's not even what we say—but how we say it—that counts. Why wouldn't every business model look to affect change by treating the customer magnificently? Because training people to be decent and nice is expensive. Hard to believe? It's the number one reason why most business organizations today don't have customer service training.

If you ask Wall Street analysts why customer service is so poor in our society today, they'll tell you that consumers don't really care about service anymore...that what the buying public is really interested in is low prices. I don't buy it and you shouldn't either. Many discount retailers have gone out of business because of poor service. Statistically, people become less sensitive to prices when service is good. Why? Again, because customers want to feel as though they count. We all need recognition.

Recognition: more important than the product

The Gallup organization polled customers around the country and discovered an amazing thing. Most people place the issue of recognition above any other issue when it comes to choosing a business brand to associate with. I use the term "brand" in this context because it's important to recognize that every business today represents a brand in its community they serve. The local pizzeria is a brand. The bakery is a brand. The car wash is a brand. The insurance agent is a brand. And, when we recognize our customers through personal contact, the mail, e-communication, phone calls, media...we're building loyalty that is more potent to our business future than any other single factor imaginable.

Recognition takes place in many forms, but the key ingredient in recognizing a customer is by simply acknowledging him or her as a fellow human being. Customer service is a constant issue for both the customer and the business. It has to be as ongoing as sweeping the floor, washing the windows, taking out the garbage, or running ads. Customer service has to infiltrate the entire business process with a cultural attitude and philosophy that's as stringent as handing out the correct change.

Buying a new customer is 10 times more costly than keeping an existing one!

Would you give up a dollar for a dime? Well, imagine business owners who would risk losing a loyal customer whose worth to the business is ten times more profitable in the short-term than attempting to acquire a new customer. The customers we own, we can own forever if we treat them properly, if we learn to say "no problem" and just say yes to their requests.

Business insanity: example number 1

A national retail chain of boating supply stores has a policy regarding gift certificates. Imagine this: You purchase a gift certificate for $100 from this chain of stores and present it as a gift. The gift's recipient takes it to one of the stores and makes a $79 purchase...only to be told that he will not receive store credit or cash for the amount remaining after the purchase.

Why is this? Well, this policy is designed to make the customer purchase more than the amount of the certificate. The store already has the money and it's earning interest in their bank account. Yet they won't permit the customer to make purchases on an as needed basis by offering store credit for the difference between the purchase and the certificate. Is this insane? *Absolutely!* Customer disservice seems to be the policy of this rather prominent chain of stores.

Ignorance is *not* bliss in marketing

Not long ago I went to a car dealership looking to purchase a minivan. I was greeted with appropriate cordiality—about to make what is typically the most expensive purchase people make next to real estate. The pleasant young saleswoman lead me to the vehicle in the showroom. Since this new generation vehicle had an electric door and a myriad of new features, I was like a kid in a candy shop. I asked questions about every aspect of the automobile. Amazingly, she didn't have a single answer at her fingertips. I got more immediate information from the sticker on the window than from the person hired to market this $30,000 product. She couldn't answer even the simplest questions. And she wasn't the least bit bothered by her ignorance. "I'll check with the manager, just wait here," was her typical response. This was told to me six times during my 20-minute perusing of this vehicle.

The saleswoman was pleasant. However, she just wasn't committed to selling her product. Rather than just walking out (which would have been a disservice to the dealership) I decided to do the right thing and tell the manager that this young lady needed a course in product knowledge. I couldn't possibly purchase the vehicle from a dealership that permitted someone without any product knowledge to attempt to sell a $30,000 product. Clearly I could handle ignorance when buying gum—maybe even when buying a shirt—but a car?! Lack of professionalism and product indifference is a clear violation of the customer service driven business.

In Joan Koob-Cannie's book, *Keeping Customers For Life*, she relates twelve barriers to *customer-driven* service. It's amazing to me that companies can justify these methods of doing business, but they are more common than companies providing even decent levels of customer service. She speaks of companies that establish policies designed for the convenience and control of the company. In these cases, the policies basically prohibit the employees from satisfying the customer.

An example she uses is one we can all relate to. If you've ever been to a hospital emergency room, surely you're aware that the policy is to present insurance information before any treatment—and before the patient is even permitted to be comforted (except for trauma or dire emergencies). This policy disallows the staff from providing the kind of care that the customer/patient longs for—especially in a situation of anxiety. Recently, Robert Wood Johnson Hospital in New Jersey began a statewide advertising campaign which offers prospective patients what they call the 10/20 rule. If a patient enters the emergency room any time of the day or night, they will be seen by a triage person within 10 minutes and a physician within 20 minutes...or the treatment is free.

Reversing the risk—a way to guarantee customer service

Let's look at another example—this one from the realm of retail jewelry. A jeweler (we'll call him "Jeweler A") in the Midwest was having a difficult time competing for engagement business. His nemesis, another local jeweler, had developed a reputation as the premier brand in the marketplace for engagement rings and diamonds. He did so by aggressive marketing and advertising to the local communities and, over time, developed a reputation for excellence—in both service and product.

The problem, then, for Jeweler A was that he had to attract customers away from a popular brand. In marketing, we look for opportunities relative to the competition (called positioning). The same is true in marketing our customer service policies. So, Jeweler A reviewed his competitor's platform and noticed a void in the selling philosophy. This void was important: Making the customer feel *totally* secure with the purchase. This was a task that would require some risk on his part but would eliminate the risk on the customer's behalf. Risk-reversal works because it acknowledges the customer as a trustworthy individual and gives the customer a sense of power in designing the transaction.

Typically, diamonds are purchased by virtue of high emotion. The minute the customer falls in love with a size, shape, or grading of a particular diamond, then the intellect takes over and fear overcomes the customer. Risk reversal removes the fear by eliminating the obstacle that creates the fear. So, Jeweler A developed a lifetime buy-back guarantee of any diamond he sold. The customer who purchases a diamond may return it for a guaranteed refund of the exact purchase price for the ownership of the diamond...in writing, backed by an insurance policy and an escrow account. The jeweler assumed the risk, and by doing so, guaranteed the customer that he was trustworthy, credible, honest, sincere, and caring. The customer could then make the purchase—knowing that this customer service policy protected them from any of the issues they feared.

When we remove the risk, we remove any fear...the fear that is the biggest factor in the failure to make sales.

"Camp" is just a four letter word

When I was 10 years old, my parents sent me off to camp. Upon my arrival, I promptly got tonsillitis and spent several days in an infirmary (with a nurse who looked like a character out of Dr. Seuss). Well, the Cat in the Hat painted my throat with a deep purple liquid and a long cotton swab. I also had a high fever and was delirious for two days. Next to me in the dark and seedy cabin was a kid who'd been bitten in the stomach by a horse. Imagine the two of us lying there all night, me moaning and him grabbing his abdomen and groaning.

On visiting day, my parents found me in the infirmary and expected that I would stay for the remaining term of my sentence. However, I *strongly* indicated my desire to leave, when they casually mentioned the fact that they had already paid for a longer stay. Dollars and sense dictated their decision to keep me in an environment that I desperately wanted to leave. I prevailed.

Every day of our lives we make decisions that commit us to products, programs, services...for periods that may go beyond our desires and needs. We do so because at the time of purchase, it seems to make sense. But does it make sense to commit to eight weeks of camp for our children when they may decide they hate it after two weeks? I'm not interested in debating the issues of stick-to-it-iveness or teaching kids responsibility. I'm only interested in treating the customer with a great deal of reverence and guaranteeing success in the relationship.

So, when my son expressed interest in attending a summer camp, I searched everywhere to find one that fit my customer service profile. And I did. This camp eliminated the rigid programs and schedules and offered kids a myriad of options...instead of an inflexible itinerary. Secondly, they assumed the financial risk. So, regardless of how many weeks I committed to, if my son hated the place, they would refund the monies paid for the unused portion of the season. And, while I signed him up for four weeks and paid for four weeks, if after one week he wasn't happy...I would get three weeks refunded—guaranteed! My decision to do business with this business was based upon their flexibility and the issue of risk reversal. Why don't more businesses make the customer feel great about the purchase decision? Because most businesses don't think the customer will demand it. In truth, this camp understands that when you guarantee something; the percentages of those who exercise the guarantee are in the two percent range. If 98 percent of the kids stay for the contracted period, their customer service policy does nothing but make them stand out in the marketplace and attract more people to their brand.

We're all in the same boat

The "no problem" method of customer service can be truly creative—even inspired. Take Jon Hurst. He owns a boat dealership. He empowers his "crew" to exercise creativity to ensure a successful relationship with customers. He clearly recognizes that success means money. But money is not what they're taught to revere. The true mission of the dealership is to create enormous goodwill, so that his primary means of marketing is his own customers. To that end, he puts their needs before the sale and has even lost sales in order to ensure a successful relationship. If people are not right for his product...he tells them. Further, he tells them what product in the marketplace might be more appropriate for them. That results in enormous goodwill.

Jon has a saleswoman named Amanda who is highly regarded by the rest of the crew at the dealership. She is an accomplished yachtswoman and holds a commercial captain's license. She deals with a great many novices who are interested in buying a boat and adapting to the boating lifestyle. Selling a beautiful boat and walking away from the sale is tempting for most people...but Amanda truly wants to create a quality experience for her customers. She keeps in touch with most of them long after the sale. She does something else—she sells *herself* with the boat. So, when the boat is delivered to the customer, she's not only there...she also sets up an appointment to teach the owner everything about the boat—navigation, docking, steering, safety, and so forth. And she commits to as many appointments as the customer feels are necessary. In truth, Amanda spends some of her free time doing what she loves—boating and teaching people about boating. This was not part of her employment contract...it was part of her own philosophy of taking customer service to an extreme.

Have it your way?

Customizing is clearly a path to delighting the customer. Remember, when we simply satisfy the customer, they will continue to look elsewhere. When we delight and excite them, they send others to us. So, when Burger King said to "have it your way," were they telling us we could have our hamburger rare? Of course not! They were simply telling us that within the context of their confined system, we could add or subtract standard ingredients, such as tomatoes or ketchup. We couldn't truly have it *our way* because their simple system wouldn't conform to true customization. So, in our business lives, we need to examine just how creative we can get for our customers. Can we give them exactly what they want...as well as maintaining our standards, systems, and profits? Most businesses have no choice if they choose to stay in business.

Let me share a story about Bob Crendola. Bob owned a very profitable clothing store. He believed in customization and creating individual experiences for each person. He believed in this so much that he customized "off the rack" suits, shirts—even ties—by not only tailoring them, but in some cases changing the structure to suit the individual. He also believed in his right as a consumer to receive customized services.

Bob always wanted a Porsche. So finally, at age forty, he decided that he could afford his Carrera. He visited area dealers and decided on a color, an interior package (customized), as well as special wheel covers. He scrupulously went over every detail with the dealer and insisted on one final issue before he would sign the papers. He didn't want the dealer to place an emblem or a sticker with their name on the car—anywhere. He refused to advertise the car dealership on his Porsche. The deal was done and the car was ordered. Bob waited impatiently for the arrival and, six weeks later, he got a call to pick up his car.

Bob was more elated than I had ever seen him before. He was like a little kid as I drove him to the dealership. He talked about the fact that, within an hour, he would be on the highway in his truly customized Porsche. When we arrived, the first thing he noticed was the small metal emblem on the trunk of the car depicting the dealer's logo. As we approached the sales manager, Bob face showed his anger and dismay. As soon as the sales manager began to speak, Bob preempted him with his own statement. "The deal is dead." He showed the salesman the emblem and stormed back to my car where he sat angrily.

I suggested that the dealer remove the emblem...but that wasn't satisfactory to Bob, who was irate that they had not listened to his request. Further, removal of the emblem would require repainting the area underneath it because paint would be removed as well in the process. It was a stalemate!

The solution was to somehow compensate Bob for the wait for a new Porsche to arrive. Clearly the dealer was in violation of the contract and now had a very vocal, angry customer. Standard customer service dictated that the dealer would have the emblem removed and to ensure Bob that repairs would be expertly done so that there would be no evidence of the emblem. However, this was offered and rejected by Bob. So, I suggested an extreme measure that would cost the dealer more but would delight Bob and keep him as a happy ambassador for the dealership. The answer was for the dealer to accept the custom car into inventory, selling it to a new customer, while loaning Bob a brand new Porsche until his custom car arrived without the emblem. The dealer weighed his options and decided that they would follow through with the plan. Bob was delighted and has shared the story with enough people to influence similar buyers to consider the dealer because of the innovative, accommodating, and extreme measures taken to correct a problem. Ultimately, "no problem" was the answer!

When we offer our customers variables and deliver upon them, we're clearly stating that they are important to us...important enough to break the mold and develop specific programs, plans, products, and services that will excite their sensibilities. Customization reflects our desire to do more than satisfy...it suggests that the customer is far more important than the standard product or service! What we're really talking about here is creativity...the kind of creativity that constantly destroys the norms, the standards, and the givens! Being creative is what has lead small companies to big market positions...and it's what the customer wants from a business.

Remembering the schoolyard bully

The first real bully I encountered was when I was starting the seventh grade. He was big, bad, and brutal. Very few kids avoided his wrath. All of the typical traits of a bully were there with Frank (I won't publish his last name because fear of reprisal still follows me around). He was physically larger and stronger than most of us. He was also arrogant, obnoxious, teasing, taunting, tormenting, and he succeeded in making every day of elementary school life miserable.

Each day during homeroom I would watch the door, hoping that the bell would ring before he arrived. That usually meant he wouldn't be in for the day and I could breathe easier—looking forward to a day without being punched or a day without the constant verbal barrage of humiliating remarks. Fighting back was not an option and civility just didn't work. He didn't understand the concepts of humanity, kindness, or cooperation. He lived to dominate and control. And so I, along with my classmates, grew accustomed to taking turns handing over our lunch money, snacks, and homework to the bully. This went on for what seemed like an eternity.

One day, however, Frank didn't show up at school. It seemed that an even tougher kid had encountered Frank on "the bridge" (an infamous location for settling disputes). He beat the tar out of Frank, leaving him badly bruised, banged up, and broken. However, while in the hospital, everyone Frank had abused called, sent cards, communicated how empathetic they were...including me! The goal was to try to get Frank to understand that, in a strange way, he had people who cared about him. We wanted him to realize that violence was a bad thing. Our goal was obvious—we wanted Frank to return from the hospital a new man! And, we fully expected that after the beating Frank took from Nick, he would be far more sensitive regarding his own boorish behavior toward others.

Amazingly...this didn't work. His behavior didn't change one single bit. He came back from his week-long stay in the hospital exactly the same as when he went in. The same evil smile, the same sadistic gestures and behavior, and the same bad attitude! So, most of us just learned to adjust to this tyrant. Much later on in life, I tried to find him in the phone book—to no avail. I'm not sure if my purpose was to confront him or just to figure out whether he still existed.

By now, you're no doubt wondering what this is all about and what it has to do with customer service. Amazingly, there are more bullies in the marketplace than we can fathom. Business people who have carried their boorish traits from the schoolyard to the business arena...audacious, obnoxious merchants who sometimes succeed in spite of their horrific behavior. Seinfeld made the Soup Nazi famous. For those of you who forget who he was, the Soup Nazi was a tyrant who happened to have the best soup in Manhattan. In fact, his product was so superior that if customers' behavior wasn't deemed acceptable to the proprietor, he bullied them out of his shop and banned them for periods of time—maybe even forever. Well, this works in a sitcom. However, it unfortunately happens in real life as well.

Brad Pitt and Jennifer Aniston walk into the store...

All too often the business owner's ego is larger than the product or service they're selling. The result is a flagrant violation of a major "just say yes" credo: Treat the customer as you would a celebrity!

Let's for a moment assume you own a retail jewelry store. Brad Pitt and Jennifer Aniston are about to get engaged. They just happen to be in your town and they decide to enter your jewelry store to buy a ring to seal the proposal. You react with amazement, enthusiasm, wonder —delighted that two such high-profile people would choose to walk into your store.

Your staff jumps over one another in order to serve them. However, you offer them a cup of coffee and a quiet private area to discuss their needs. You go to any lengths to "get to know them" and to get them to feel good about you. You're so enamored with these two customers that you offer them all sorts of guarantees. You ask them questions about their lifestyle—looking for an intimate connection with them. When Jennifer expresses interest in a bracelet as well as the ring, you gently place it on her wrist, smiling into her eyes, recognizing that contact is very powerful.

"If there's anything you have in mind that you don't see in the cases, I'll bring out a designer and a sketch pad, and we'll bring your vision to life—no obligation, of course." You're certain never to lose eye contact as you offer her yet another bagel, coffee, etc. After all, she's Jennifer Aniston. Oh, and Brad wants a bracelet (it's her gift to him). You bring out a tray of bracelets, but he doesn't see any that strike his fancy. You offer to send some over to his hotel room later in the day because they're in a hurry. As they're readying to leave, you hand them your card with an intricately wrapped chocolate truffle, and politely ask them to fill out the 20-second survey, so that you may send them private, special offers along the way. They comply.

The very next day, the thank you note goes out to them...whether they bought something or not. In addition, a copy of the "Hottest Trends in Jewelry Fashion" article from *Cosmopolitan* or *Vogue* accompanies the thank you note. Then you sit down with your staff at your R.O.C.K. (Roundtable Of Competitive Knockouts) meeting first thing Monday morning. You ask each team member for their ideas on how to excite the customer so much that they feel celebrated each and every time they visit your business.

You, of course, review Jennifer and Brad's visit to your store and ask how ou could have made it better—for them and for you. Recognize that no suggestion should be met with negativity from the boss...any comment is worthy of consideration.

Eventually, you tell your staff that every customer *is* Brad Pitt and Jennifer Aniston...each and every one. And, every customer must be met with the same level of excitement as celebrated guests.

Marketing, after all, is not simply creating communication...it's creating attitudes. An attitude conveys your philosophy of doing business while it adds up to building awareness and loyalty—the two major issues in business today.

So, the next time "Brad and Jennifer" walk through your door, your system will be in place based upon the knowledge that as celebrated people, they will make or break you in the marketplace—one customer at a time!

Business insanity: example number 2

Don owned a local pharmacy in my town. Even though he was a relatively young man (about 35 years old) he had an old attitude toward customers. This attitude included being suspicious of young people and generally aloof toward everyone.

I lived near the pharmacy and it was very convenient for me to shop there. And I did...until I'd had enough of his insanity. On one occasion, Don's air conditioning had gone out on a particularly hot day. As I waited for a prescription, I asked why he hadn't gone out and bought some fans in order to cool off himself, his employees, and his customers. His retort was short and sarcastic, "would you like to pay for the fans?" I let it ride. The next time I was in his store, he was busy placing price stickers on deodorant as I waited to pick up a prescription. After about five minutes, I asked him, "May I pick up my prescription and pay you?" He finished some of the stickers while I remained at the counter, fuming. He then ungraciously took care of my needs.

At what point do we react? It depends on the level of convenience the business affords us. The breaking point for me was the next visit, when my then six-year-old son desperately needed to use a bathroom. I asked if he could use the facility and Don responded by telling me to use the pizzeria next door. At that point, I left and drove the ten minutes to his competitor. I asked the owner about the level of service I could expect as a customer. When I was satisfied that the service would be far more compelling and attentive, I had the new pharmacist call and transfer the prescriptions.

However, I also did something else which was important. I wrote a very aggressive letter to Don describing the revenue he lost just from treating me poorly. Then, I calculated my impact on friends and neighbors and suggested the potential revenue that I could affect regarding his business. The numbers were staggering and more powerful than merely describing my hurt feelings. The bottom line: Within three years, he was gone.

Everyone is a little afraid

Civility is a forgotten concept in business today. I believe that the issue of civility will be one of the most important business principles as the millennium forces us to do business with faceless entities—powered into our lives by technology. Because fear is such a great factor in choosing who we do business with, it's important to understand that fear can be overcome with simple communication.

What is it that we're all afraid of? First, we're afraid of being taken advantage of. We're terrified that we'll be duped by some business that only wants our money and could care less about a relationship. We're afraid of placing ourselves in the unenviable position of being humiliated by our own ignorance. Well, the very same entity that removes us from human contact can be used to provide us with the proper ammunition to transact business...with less fear. The Internet allows us to research all of our purchases for quality, integrity, price, features, benefits, and options. So, while we may not choose to do business for major purchases directly with an Internet provider, we can get all the necessary information for making a good buying decision when we visit the seller in person. By the year 2010, many of our purchases will be done with nontraditional "e-businesses." For now, the Internet is evolving as a primary resource for researching the obstacles that create fear on the consumer's part.

The average consumer knows little about most higher-ticket products or services they buy. Therefore, we rely upon the integrity of honest business people to hold our hands and walk us through the purchase so that we get what we need at a reasonable price. In addition, we want more than just what we need—We're all looking for enhancement in the purchases we make. These may be value-added components, such as additional guarantees, warranties, add-ons, and so forth. Or, these components may be as intangible as a handshake, a smile, or a promise from the business that you'll be taken care of.

When Allstate began using the motto, "You're in good hands at Allstate," it was written to remove the obstacle that exists typically in the sale of insurance: fear. By communicating to the customer that "you're in good hands" and repeating that message consistently, the result is a feeling of trust on the part of the prospects who are uneducated and wary of buying expensive insurance...the ultimate intangible.

We overcome fear with love

We need to recognize that when we address the issue of *fear*, we also address the issue of *love*. (By love, I am not referring to the romantic kind, but rather the warm and fuzzy sense of being cared about as an individual.) Both go hand in hand in influencing buying decisions. Extreme customer service is based upon the principle that love must replace fear in the seller/buyer relationship. Here's how it's done.

When we approach a purchase decision that is *desire* based (unlike *need*-based purchases, such as soap, shaving cream, milk, eggs, keys, etc.), we do so with a strong emotional sensibility. Let's take clothing, for example. Clearly we need to wear clothing to protect us from the elements. But, beyond the pragmatic side of the purchase is a personal desire to look good. So, we enter the clothing store with preconceived notions about what we desire to become. For many people, clothing is a strong extension of personality. For others, it's a fantasy on what they would like to be. And, for many of us, clothing is designed for simple comfort and casual style. But, in all cases, the desire is to look good and feel good. Remember, the primary need on the part of customers is recognition. Therefore, the customer needs to be acknowledged for his or her individuality.

What's the fear in shopping for clothing? Typically, the fear is twofold. Do the clothes truly look good on me? Am I paying the right price for them? The reason that so many people shop with a friend or even a group of friends for clothing is because the salesperson might not be honest with the customer on his or her appearance.

How is that overcome? As a customer, you have a right to be skeptical regarding the motivation of the salesperson. As a seller, you have a responsibility to be an expert in your knowledge of the product and your aesthetic sensibilities. If you truly influence buying decisions, you need to convey an honest, educated point of view relative to the customer's desire to look good in the clothing they select.

You need to offer the customer a variety of options that would better suit them if, in your opinion, they are heading down the wrong road. This sometimes means suggesting less expensive choices that are more complimentary to the customer.

For example, when I arrived at Nordstrom to purchase a dark blue suit for a wedding, I was fearful because I was shopping alone. However, the fear was allayed immediately when a very attractive saleswoman spent a few moments asking me about the reason for my purchase. She didn't begin the relationship by showing me suits on a rack. She asked why I was purchasing a suit, what color I wanted (and why), how committed was I to a single breasted jacket, how often I planned to wear the suit, who was getting married, was I one of the members of the bridal party, and so on and so forth. She also asked if the wedding was black tie optional (which it was) and why I had decided not to simply rent a tuxedo. This was amazing! Here was a salesperson who was more interested in getting to know me—my likes and dislikes, my concerns, my sense of style, and my lifestyle needs—than she was in making a sale. She even questioned the validity of my purchasing a suit rather than renting a tuxedo. What's that all about? It's about a commitment to creating a quality experience for me, the customer. That quality experience begins by doing something extraordinary...getting to know the customer before attempting to make the sale. It's a critical issue. The importance of getting to know me first as an individual was the best approach in getting to know me as a potential customer. And, psychologically, the fear dissipated in the process. In fact, not only did I no longer feel apprehensive, I felt nurtured, taken care of, appreciated...even recognized! The truth was that no matter whatever advice she offered to me, I was totally receptive toward. Extreme customer service had softened the sale to the degree that my fear was truly replaced by love.

Let me share another example of how love replaces fear in a sale. I accompanied a friend of mine recently who is passionate about antiques. An avid collector and reseller (on eBay.com), he and I walked into a little house of antiques in a quaint town in the south. The genteel, silver-haired proprietor greeted us not with the usual, "Can I help you," but rather with, "May I offer you gentlemen a cup of coffee or tea?" My friend chose to abstain, while I accepted her gracious offer. The coffee arrived in a china cup on a small antique tray with a little pitcher of milk, a silver spoon, a dish of sugar, and packets of sugar substitute. Three chocolate-dipped biscotti accompanied the coffee.

I was sold, won over, in love, and in awe of her charm and ingenuity. I hunted through the store and made a modest purchase of a simple little carving that I truly liked...but probably would never have bought had she not been so gracious and unassuming. It turned out that she was an expert and my friend ended up spending hundreds of dollars without sipping any coffee. She approached us with a small, friendly gesture and developed an instant rapport that created trust, credibility, and even a slight sense of obligation to purchase something...anything! The standard fare of fear that usually accompanies entering an unknown environment with products that clearly have little or unknown comparable value was banished immediately by her endearing presence.

Reading between the lines

The Boat House restaurant sits on a small barrier reef resort island just north of Atlantic City. The window of opportunity to make a living exists between Memorial Day and Labor Day—for the most part. The biggest problem for the owner is turning tables during the busy season. After all, you can't force people to eat quickly and vacate their tables...and those waiting on the line can get awfully persnickety. Typically, businesses do nothing for their patrons in waiting, and there's a fair amount of attrition...so that up to half of those waiting leave before reaching their table. If you calculate the losses, they can amount to an enormous total. Short of building a bigger restaurant (which they eventually did), the solution lied in creating a feeling of nurture and love...and obligation on the part of the customer to remain in line long enough to be seated, served, and charged.

The solution was so simple that it has been adopted by national chains like Outback. A server tends to those in line with complimentary appetizers and soft drinks which are offered to everyone waiting. Statistically, though 90 percent of those waiting will partake of the food and drink, none of them will order less food when they finally arrive at their table. Amazingly, more than 90 percent remain in line because of the service, good feelings, and a sense of obligation—Who could ask for anything more? What patrons remember about the restaurant is this issue. Yes, the food is good, the service is friendly, the atmosphere pleasant...but the experience of receiving something free is the singular issue that is recalled by all.

Truffles, anyone?

Simms is an upscale jewelry store with an eclectic collection of platinum, diamonds, gold, the most renowned names in watches, Tiffany jewelry, and a host of other rather exclusive products and services. The business has a long history of success—entering the third generation of proprietorship. The experience of shopping at Simms is quite lovely. Beautiful music is piped in. Sophisticated expert salespeople are sincere and attentive...not pushy. The products are decidedly targeted to the upscale clientele. Services, such as gift wrapping, free shipping, and additional guarantees are standard. However, if you ask the customers who have shopped at Simms for the one thing that they remember above all else, the majority will answer, "truffles." Not gold, diamonds, watches, or pearls—but truffles! Why is this? Because at the entrance (which is also the exit), a beautiful crystal dish of extraordinary truffles is a fixture. Fresh exotic truffles. Simms does a lot of things right, but their extreme gesture is the dish of truffles that is constantly replenished. And, they encourage (if not insist) that all of their customers partake of this extravagant indulgence. It's what extreme customer service is about...giving the customer something completely beyond the norm, something completely unexpected.

A cappuccino with your haircut?

Daniel's Salon is also decidedly upscale. Located in an affluent suburb of New York City, it caters to a clientele that appreciates those "extras." In fact, the customers not only appreciate the value added components of the experience—they expect them. Interestingly, when we treat our customers well, we elevate their expectations. This can pose a problem. We must always be proactive and creative in stretching our imaginations in order to continually delight spoiled customers. Daniel's began to create an extreme service story by picking up its customers in a limousine. Then, they would have an employee run out to get cappuccino, coffee, brioche, bagels, and so forth.

After a while, Daniel decided that it was worthwhile to install a cappuccino bar in his salon. With increased business, he took advantage of an open space when the store next door vacated the mini mall. He broke through the wall, adding about twice the square footage of his original salon. The new space was designed with a walnut and brass bar which served as the "cafe" for the business. Of course, the cafe was there to provide complimentary refreshments for the clientele. But after a while, customers would show up to buy a cup of cappuccino or a croissant, without wanting their hair cut.

Daniel resisted at first, but then decided to create an expanded menu which included sandwiches, salads, fruit smoothies, specialty foods, candies, and pastries. Daniel then petitioned the town to allow tables inside and outside, as well as making the modest adjustments in order to operate a noncooking food service business within his salon. What resulted was an explosion in sales and profits—with the food side actually outpacing the sales from the salon. His concept of extreme service remained the same—and his salon customers were offered "continental" fare as a complimentary service. Beyond that, most of his hair customers became food customers as well, visiting the salon/cafe in between appointments because the offerings were so unusual and special for the area. What started out to be a creative gesture became a bigger business—all by virtue of thinking about how extreme customer service issues would make his customers feel. The car service remains an option for customers (mostly older women who prefer not to drive or park) and is a fixture in Daniel's business personality.

Cookies for your car

Ron Friedland bought a Toyota from an area dealer recently. He was happy with the service he received. He loved the car and felt good about the deal he made. If you ask Ron today why he's gone back to the same dealer three times for new leases he'll reply with all sincerity, "It's because of the cookies."

Ron's not being facetious. He truly likes the product and the dealer. But what Ron really appreciates is the wonderful tin of cookies he receives from the salesperson after signing a new car lease. When Ron expressed his thanks to Rich, the salesman, Rich could've replied, "well, we do that for all our customers," and he'd be right. But what Rich did was to create a simple little system that shipped the tin of cookies every three months. Ron gets his treat four times a year now instead of once. Rich knows that unless the product falls from grace or Ron is wooed by another car, another dealer, a better deal...he owns Ron forever because of some tins of cookies. I know this sounds simplistic, but that's because it is. The smallest, simplest gestures of friendship and recognition create loyal, dedicated customers.

5 easy pieces?

The no problem philosophy of doing business was never more obviously exemplified than in the legendary movie with Jack Nicholson titled *Five Easy Pieces.* The story revolves around a man who rejects his intellectual past, including his impressive performances as a concert pianist. In leaving behind his family, he revolts against his background and his culture in search of some meaning to his life. He eventually takes a job as a laborer on an oil rig and begins a life that is totally opposite the one he left behind. The story is an intense view of a man caught between two worlds—repelled by both.

In an infamous scene, he stops at a diner with his girlfriend and another couple from their working class world. Nicholson's character wants an order of dry whole wheat toast. The waitress, a sour-faced, middle aged discontent, reacts in a nasal, whiny drone, "we don't have no side orders of whole wheat toast." Nicholson, bewildered, asks if they have chicken salad—to which the waitress responds in the affirmative. He further asks if they can make a chicken salad sandwich on whole wheat toast...again the response is yes.

"So, what you're saying is that you have whole wheat bread back there in the kitchen...and you can make a chicken salad sandwich on whole wheat toast, but you can't give me a side order of the whole wheat toast?" The waitress again reacts, "That's right, we don't have side orders of whole wheat toast, do you want the chicken salad sandwich or not?"

Nicholson responds, "I'll tell you what, give me a chicken salad sandwich on whole wheat toast dry...then take the chicken salad and stick it!"

We live by rules. When we ask people who are not in decision making modes to make simple decisions, the system falls down. The waitress didn't have any abilities beyond order taking. She was not empowered to make simple changes because there was no training for simple changes. What's worse, she failed to make any sense...like the pizza parlor that charges more for four slices of pizza than it does for a whole pie of eight slices. There is no logic in these policies, but they are policies and we place policies before patrons all the time. The only answer to any reasonable request is **no problem**. For businesses with policies that are unalterable, consider that you'll be living with your policies a lot longer than you'll be enjoying your customers.

Chapter 2

Unhappy Customers Don't Always Yell Back...They Just Stop Coming

"How'my'doin?" asked Mayor Koch when he was in charge of New York. He asked it often...and he was serious. Ed Koch understood that in terms of constituents or customers, no news is bad news. Why is this? Most people will quietly seethe, burning up with hostility and anger. They'll keep quiet until election time—and by then, it's too late to win them back. Customers are exactly the same. If you don't have a good understanding of your relationship with them then you run the serious risk of losing them. Serious commitment to extreme customer service begins with the commitment made by the top management, owner, or director. The process of getting customers to communicate begins by understanding that you as a business manager must institute a strategy and a program that will keep the customers involved in your business.

Jay Sprechler, author of *When America Does It Right*, studied customer service programs of some of the nation's top companies listed by *Fortune* magazine. Sprechler created a diagram which prioritized how companies "own" customers. His concept was to establish a committee within any organization that dealt with customers which he called a "customer action council." From that starting point, he instituted the following issues that frameworked the program.

- Calculate what it costs to develop a customer service program.
- Establish an ongoing customer information system.
- Demonstrate the management commitment toward customer service.

- Train all personnel in customer-driven skills (empower them to be creative).
- Set goals and determine performance measures.
- Take care of the team through incentives and motivational issues.
- Train frontline employees to put the customer first (before their own needs).
- Communicate the goals of the business and establish standards and recognize achievements.
- Motivate all levels of employees to "think customer" and provide value-added service.
- Train all employees to be "customer champions."
- Establish a continuous improvement network.
- Create an employee information loop so that all employees know what everyone is doing.
- Provide training in "creative problem solving" for salespeople (from the maintenance person to the sales manager).
- Track and measure the program for on-going improvement.
- Recognize and reward performance and celebrate, celebrate, celebrate!

These issues all relate to common sensibilities. When we look at extreme behavior toward the customer, we recognize that without the customer there would be no business. Secondly, recognize that because everyone is a customer, we want outstanding treatment for ourselves *as* customers. Understanding that, we want to give outstanding treatment to those we serve.

Many of your customers will not yell back. This isn't because they're afraid of the businesses they work with, but for many reasons. This includes the fact that our culture has created a cynical customer base, and customers don't expend the time and the energy necessary to tell you how poorly you treat them. Further, for those who do, very little satisfaction is offered...even by major marketers.

Airlines need to be grounded

Airlines are notorious for horrible customer service. I was talking to a friend about a recent trip he took. He told me horror stories about his trip. Here is his story:

"I had booked five tickets to Albuquerque. One of those travelling with me is physically challenged and I paid about 30 percent extra to secure tickets that did not require changing planes in St. Louis. A week or so before the trip, I was notified that the return flight would indeed require a change of planes. I was offered no explanation, no discount, or no apology—after all, this is an airline. So, I wrote to the president of the airline asking for some explanation...and never heard a word back.

"On the way out to Albuquerque, the plane stopped to add passengers in St. Louis and we were told that we could stretch our legs during the brief layover. My eight-year-old son and 15-year-old daughter wanted to wander into the airport for a few minutes. I accompanied them and was abruptly told that I would have to wait on the line along with those boarding for the continuation of the flight. When I suggested that we would then return to the plane to join the rest of our party, I was abruptly stopped and the door to the entryway was shut. I asked the flight attendant why I was being treated so poorly. She told me to keep my mouth shut and that she wasn't interested in hearing my complaint. I was so stunned that I could barely react. When I came to my senses, I asked another flight attendant who brushed me off with equal indifference."

Needless to say, this seemed like the policy of the airline, otherwise it couldn't possibly have happened. Is it possible that companies have errant employees who act outside of the corporate strategy? Yes...but not two on the same plane 68 percent. The airline doesn't hear most of the complaints because customers feel the indifference, making it seem futile to complain. So, they drift off to alternative carriers whenever possible, even though the industry has no care, nurturing, or concern on the part of the management or the employees. Look at the statistics and the pending legislation which is designed to control the abuses heaped upon the public by airlines.

Because upper-level commitment is critical to the success of a customer-driven philosophy, management must establish rules and create an environment in which the same level of concern is given to the employees that is being requested by the employees. In Joan Koob Cannie's book, *Keeping Customers for Life*, she suggests that "there isn't a single case where quality developed from a bottom up approach. It is clear that the CEO can never walk away from maintaining a direct, highly-visible, and pervasive involvement in quality."

A quote worth repeating: In an American Institute For Quality Control report to industry leaders in 1996, they stated that 68 percent of those customers surveyed would leave a business relationship because of an act of indifference on the part of an employee.

Government studies conducted by the American Association of Advertising Agencies suggest that only four customers in 100 will complain. One of the reasons people won't complain is because they feel that no one will listen. When we listen, we create family, when we turn a deaf ear, we create adversaries who speak harshly about our business to others. That's tantamount to distributing literature that trashes our own business...why would anyone do that?

CitiCorp Savings of California has an edict: "Service excellence is a nonnegotiable requirement. It is no more an option for the organization than is operational control. It is an essential and nonnegotiable element in our future success. It is up to every manager to actively and visibly support the achievement of service standards, and it is up to every manager to coach employees in being sensitive to service in all aspects of our business—service to our customer as well as service to each other..."

Have you been to a bank lately? Fleet Bank, for example, charges service fees if you need to speak to a customer service representative, rather than use its automated system of inquiry. Have you stood in the roped areas waiting to be treated with grave indifference by an uncaring, unsmiling, unhappy employee? Probably more often than not, I would imagine. Organizations truly believe that price and location offset service. So much so that many companies don't consider customer service programs because of the cost!

Quick Chek Food Stores, an innovative chain of over 100 stores in the Northeast, has a unique organizational chart. This chart is called the "Upside-Down Flow Chart," and on it, the customer is at the top and the president and CEO are at the bottom. This defining document is a top down approach, recognizing that if customers have options (regardless of price and location) they will exercise those options once they've been annoyed once too often. By recognizing that the customer is the true boss, Quick Chek keeps customer service at the core of its mission.

If you call Bell Atlantic and require a live person to communicate with, you'll get a pleasant individual who will answer your questions efficiently. They will end the conversation by asking you a question: "Would you say that you've been treated well during this conversation?" You may answer any way you like, but most people reply positively. This is a good example of friendly service. The question is not just a ploy...but a policy established by Bell Atlantic to find out if they're going to retain you as a customer. Statistically, they measure the responses and can then project customer retention. How else would they know if they're well perceived? We need to find out what we're doing right and how we're impacting the customer. Customers rarely yell back when they are treated poorly...again, they just don't come back. Remember: You want products that *never* come back and customers that *always* come back.

Have you heard from your customers lately? It's getting late and they haven't spoken to you in a while...maybe it's time to act and ask!

Do the right thing

Spike Lee said it. Westinghouse said it as well. In their corporate position, Westinghouse stated, "Total quality means meeting customer requirements by doing the right things right, the first time." The only exception I would make to that statement is that it's not enough to simply meet the customers' requirements—we must exceed them. Extreme customer service begins where customer service ends. Remember this adage: "Satisfied customers look elsewhere, delighted customers send others to you." (I'll repeat it throughout the book.) When we speak about "doing the right thing," we're talking primarily about giving customers tangible reasons to think about us between visits. That requires us to be top of mind by becoming top of heart. Cannie, author of *Keeping Customers For Life*, created a triangle of quality which outlines the issue of customer service maintenance. You can see it on page 36.

Without asking the customer their response, all the promotional statements in the world fall flat. When a nursing home promotes their company as providing "excellent care," what do they mean? Most companies use useless cliches that have no meaning. What is excellent care without the customer's point of view? Even the most prominent banking institutions, credit card companies, and others talk about quality as

The Triangle of Quality

Requirements:
Customer satisfaction.
Stockholder value.
Employee satisfaction.
Public approval.

QUALITY

Imperatives:
Customer orientation.
Human resource excellence.
Product/process leadership.
Management leadership.

if it were in and of itself definable. What is quality? How do companies define their own use of the word?

In truth, quality is a vaporous issue. The only time it becomes tangible is when we give the customer a credible list of issues that they can take away from the experience and put in a jar, so to speak. If companies really want to offer a quality experience, then the dialogue between the company and the customer must be nonstop.

In *Customer Loyalty* by Jill Griffin, she looks to define the customer. The definition, she states, of a customer is "a person who becomes accustomed to buying from you." Without a strong track record of repeat purchases, this person is not your customer; he or she is your "buyer." A true customer is "grown" over time.

If we look at what makes a good customer, we learn that customer loyalty and what I call "customer-love" is the strongest bond we can have with our "strategic partner." If we look at the customer as a partner, we need to recognize that true customers rely upon us as much as we rely upon them. Think about it. Customers are people who come to us repeatedly for goods and services. They look within our organizations to buy as many products as they can use...and they become ambassadors for us in gaining new customers. Customers who love us cannot be easily swayed away from the relationship.

The customer as a friend

Let's look at how customers become our friends...and stay friends. Would you abandon a friendship that works on all levels just because someone else came along and said "play with me instead"? Rather, friendships are based upon trust, value, compatibility. We choose our friends because they make the most sense to us. They meet our needs and requirements in terms of philosophy, interests, demeanor—even physical appearance. We choose our business relationships in much the same manner.

The reason we are drawn to a particular business relationship begins with the public persona—the marketing, advertising, public relations. We choose our alliance based upon our first impressions, recommendations, and referrals. In the case of first impressions, we make a value judgement from the communications we receive. When we see an ad that portrays an image, we make a value judgment based upon that communication. When we hear a radio commercial, see a TV spot, receive a direct mail solicitation, or view a billboard, we are digesting and processing the information we need to decide upon entering into the relationship. Once we feel comfortable enough, we act. Now, sometimes we act because of greed, which in the case of choosing a business is price or value-added promotions. In the case of a friendship, it might be choosing who to meet because they have offered you the best seats at the ballgame. In all relationships, we are wooed by many factors.

Let's assume we respond to the advertising because it relates to us, our lifestyle, our aesthetic needs, even our sense of greed. We can only be fooled once. If the experience is a positive one, the "romance" can begin. The romance of business relationships takes place once we're won over by the initial offering (marketing).

Now, we've experienced the relationship and it feels good. What's going to keep us committed? Consistency. In Jill Griffin's book, *Customer Loyalty*, she looks to one of the classic examples of customer-driven comebacks in this country: Harley Davidson. The company, now in its 96th year of business, had a 63 percent market share just six years ago on its ninetieth birthday. 100,000 people attended the celebration—all loyal friends of Harley Davidson. 18,000 members of the Harley Davidson Owners Group were there...and hotel rooms were sold out within 60 miles of the event. The company enjoys that rare gift of customer love. The "family" of customers consider themselves part of the Harley Davidson commune. It isn't a product, it's a part of community.

Recognizing that "community" is a key issue in evolving to extreme customer service, Harley Davidson cultivates its community through its dealer networks, mailings, associations, cultural products, and commitment to excellence. It's an amazing phenomenon and one that truly reflects a monumental effort on the part of management.

How does a company seemingly doomed for failure create such customer loyalty? During the early 1980s, Harley Davidson was a classic example of a failing company. The company was the only American manufacturer left in the production of motorcycles, having been outperformed and outmarketed by Asian manufacturers. Its impending doom gave rise to incredible creativity. It began with reinventing the manufacturing process and upgrading the quality issues to compete with Japanese companies who were light years ahead of Harley Davidson in production and performance. Halfway into the 80s, Harley had begun to perform more credibly in terms of quality. With production issues on the road to resolution, Harley Davidson began to look at its customers. Things had changed in the past decade and motorcycle riders no longer fit the same profile they had in the past.

Long gone were the days of the 22-year-old Brandoesque character who rode into town in a leather jacket with dust at his trail. For one thing, the average price of a Harley Davidson exceeded $10,000 and few young riders could afford the ticket. The goal was to entice the right customers back to an American-made motorcycle, one that had captured a piece of our national imagination for decades. What Harley Davidson did was to identify the emerging Harley owner and cater to his or her specific needs and wants.

Extreme customer service begins by recognizing the behavior of the customer and then behaving correctly to that customer. In the case of Harley Davidson, the old perceptions of motorcycle riders needed to be shelved and replaced with the new Harley customer—a middle-aged rider from the middle to upscale marketplace who uses their machine to enhance their lifestyle—indeed to add some excitement and adventure to ordinary lives.

The H.O.G. (Harley Owner's Group) are fiercely loyal customers. And, like the best customers possible, they are constantly referring others to the brand. As evidenced by surveys, Harley owners consider their choice to be the only choice for motorcycles. How does this kind of customer loyalty evolve?

If we look at research that speaks to the passions, concerns and questions that customers are asking, we see that we are a schizophrenic society, as Watts Wacker, noted futurist, suggests. We say one thing, but we act in another way. What we want as consumers is to be safe—while being totally excited. We want a strong sense of community and we want those we do business with to be experts in their disciplines.

Building customer loyalty

Customer loyalty is a cumulative issue. We begin by understanding that customers begin as skeptics. Once we do, the following steps will begin to get customers to love us:

1. Helping customers overcome suspicion. The first approach a customer makes is done with much suspicion. The first impression a customer has is sometimes the last impression the customer has—if they're not pleased, they're gone. We overcome their suspicious nature by anticipating the questions they have and providing answers and solutions before the questions are raised.

For example, in the case of a hardware store owner who's focusing on the do-it-yourselfer...the hardware store owner recognizes that at least 65 percent of those who enter the store don't have the experience to complete the job. Many of them don't even know what tools to request or what materials are necessary. This fear is an impediment in creating customers. Extreme customer service policies would include a review of the project, a guarantee that the materials purchased will do the job or they can be returned, and a pledge to the customer to be available by phone for the hand holding that will help the customer complete the job. By offering these issues up front, suspicions turn into solutions.

2. Establishing yourself as the expert. Trust and customer loyalty go hand in hand. Establishing trust requires the customer's acknowledgment that you are the expert. If you assume the customer knows what they want, you will fail. As the expert, it's your job to establish a relationship based upon the premise that your experience, history, and knowledge will allow you to direct the customer to the right product or service. Customers are usually insecure and want to be in the hands of an expert. If your product knowledge is lacking, get your education up to speed before you begin handling customers' needs.

3. Create a sense of community. Saturn has broken many molds in automobile marketing. Loyal customers are more important to Saturn than units sold. That's certainly the message they've imparted. While we can cynically suspect that the customer loyalty campaign is insincere, they've managed to create a strong customer base that keeps coming back. They did so by dispensing with standards sales methods and focusing on the customer...not the car. The car's features and benefits are less pronounced than the customers. So, we get a sense of the product by gaining insight into the types of customers who buy the product. The commercials focus on lifestyle, commitments, quality, and personalities...the car comes later.

The truth is that it's a brilliant approach when the product lives up to the lifestyle. In the case of Saturn they fell short because they didn't recognize the need on the part of their loyal customers for a bigger product. The community center was just a bit too small to satisfy the community. The concept, though, is correct. Create a community for your customer by including them in the entire process of ownership. Letters, follow-up phone calls, a newsletter, postcards, database mailings, and events are all part of how communities thrive.

Make the customer a salesperson

When the Toyota dealership sends the customer cookies—not once but four times a year—they're making their customer a salesperson for their brand. Because of the old adage that word of mouth is the best form of promotion, we must remember that our existing customers can outsell our salespeople. Why not give them incentives to tell their friends and families about the product or service? You could award a commission, an incentive, a prize, a percentage discount, an appearance in a future ad, or a free accessory! The customer who becomes an advocate is the best customer service representative you have...and extreme customer service happens when you have extremely happy customers.

Make your team members managers of their own business

Think about it. What if each member of your staff—be they two or 22—were in business for themselves, under the umbrella of your business? What if they could make decisions based upon exciting and delighting the customer without regard to any policy of exclusion? The idea is to make the salesperson into the "customer comfort manager." Anything that the salesperson needs to do to make the customer comfortable is permissable...anything that is not illegal, immoral, unethical, or unprofitable (sometimes you can even compromise on profitability to create a loyal customer). The Customer Comfort Manager has the responsibility to do anything that will create a comfortable, loyal, delighted customer. First, you need your own business card (Nordstrom does it), regardless of your position with the firm. Second, you need to recognize that you have complete control over making not only the sale but the contract. Once you engage a customer and connect them to your business you've signed a contract to exceed their needs from that point forward. So, the empowerment you have as a partner to the firm also carries with it a responsibility to care for the customer in profound ways.

Tom Peters in his *Circle of Innovation* suggests that business managers and salespeople visit every client, both past and present, to ensure that they are loyal. What you may find is that loyalty has ceased to exist among many of them because of lack of contact, care, commitment, or concern. The strategy of staying connected ensures that even when we don't hear from them, they hear from us. Dissatisfied customers can be wooed back and satisfied customers can be brought back to our brand once again. Do the work over if it was done without exceeding the customer's needs.

Take Everett McKenzie. He's a gifted carpenter and runs a moderately successful business. Everett began to be proactive after his father left the business. He finally had the autonomy to follow his own heart and mind in securing his future as head of McKenzie Construction.

Everett decided that he would call all of the past customers who he had not heard from in seven years. He chose seven years, because he knew that typically he had repeat projects during that period of time on the average. Because he served both commercial and residential customers, Everett McKenzie called customers and found some astonishing things. About 10 percent of those he reintroduced himself to were not happy with the work they had received from his firm. That wasn't bad, just 10 percent and Everett was willing to write it off to the fact that every company probably has about a 10 percent dissatisfaction rate and disgruntled customer were those who would never be satisfied. But, upon further investigation, Everett began to understand that most of his past customers weren't delighted either. Many were basically satisfied, but many felt that there were areas of the work that could have been done better, faster or cheaper.

Everett decided to do a recall—not unlike any manufacturer when it is discovered that a product has faults in it. Everett offered each customer who had areas of discontent a free fix-it! In each case, he guaranteed that he would revisit their home or building and repair, replace, or fix what was perceived as being less than excellent. An amazing thing happened. About 30 percent of the customers from the past invited him back to look at new projects they had for him...and only 5 percent of those projects from the past called him back for repairs. The very fact that he had asked the customers if they were happy and guaranteed their happiness at no extra cost, gained him a third of those customers back with active projects. The brilliant notion of guaranteeing past work and reinventing future work with unheralded guarantees catapulted Everett's business from $5,000,000 to $15,000,000 in less than five years.

When you remember that quiet customers are dangerous liabilities, you can begin to reach out to your past customers whom you haven't heard from in order to secure your future with them. Those who have remained even mildly dissatisfied will stifle your growth and inhibit your ability to use them as active advocates for your business.

Is there anything you won't do in order to succeed?

Is there anything you won't do for the customer (outside of blatantly unprofitable, immoral, illegal, or unethical issues)? During a seminar I was giving, I asked this question. Several people in the audience raised their hands with trivial answers. At the risk of sounding arrogant, I suggested to them that they might be better served in attending a different seminar because I feel so strongly about this issue that I don't think they would have learned anything. Think about your business and your customer. A good creative exercise is to think about your business as your customer. When you recognize that your business is, in fact, your customer, you're on the road to saying yes to customer requests.

The following story is a favorite of mine to mention because it is so typical. A friend and I went to the small town of New Hope, Pennsylvania. We had stolen an afternoon for a sanity break on a beautiful spring day. The tourist town was uncrowded because it was a weekday and the streets were quiet. During the afternoon, I needed to use a restroom...bad. I encountered sign after sign in the windows of the stores that blared "Restrooms are for patrons only." Finally, out of desperation, I hurried into a casual pizza restaurant. I was confronted by the owner, who asked if I would like to be seated. I honestly told him that I needed a restroom—he told me back that I should pay attention to his sign. I told him that I was in marketing and I would give him enormously valuable advice for free: "Take down your sign and replace it with one that reads: 'Restrooms are for anyone who needs them.'" Statistically, I related, he will not be taken advantage of and the good will would eventually increase his business—just by posting that sign. He allowed me the use of the restroom and I bgrudgingly bought a soda on the way out. I doubt that he ever removed the sign, but at least I tried.

In the case of this restaurant, there were things they *wouldn't* do, even if they would succeed to a greater degree. What's your issue? What won't you change?

Either you or a competitor won't be in business in 5 years

This isn't a threat, it's a fact that 2.3 trillion dollars of the United States' gross national product comes from small businesses. Two out of three high-tech jobs are within the framework of small businesses. Some thrive, but half of the new start-ups fail. There are many reasons, but one critical factor remains true throughout the business arena—relationship integrity. We've all heard of product integrity—looking at the product or service relative to the competition. We've all heard of competitive pricing. We've certainly all heard of relationship marketing, right? Well, the majority of small businesses today have little or no service-sense. So, walk outside your store, look to your left and your right, because one of you three will eventually fail.

Unless you're willing to evaluate the strength of the connection that exists between you and your customer; unless you're willing to risk reducing profits in order to increase loyalty; unless you're willing to create a powerful value-added selling proposition; and unless you can guarantee excellence, you're doomed to failure.

"You're either on the bus or you're off the bus."

Tom Wolfe, noted nonfiction novelist, made this statement famous in his *Electric Kool Aid Acid Test.* Literally, you're either with us or you're not! It's a good question to ask your team members, partners, and every other level of employment at your company. Extreme customer service begins by imbedding your people with the notion that we're all travelling down the same road together. If we are truly customer-driven, even on a bad day after a fight with your wife, girlfriend, husband, sister, or otherwise, the company policy toward customers must remain seamless.

The best way to keep employees motivated to delight customers is to constantly provide positive reinforcement and incentives...and to let them know that you ask customers about their experience with the company. If you ask customers about their experience with individual team members, this will keep everyone honest. If an employee chooses not to be on the bus, then he or she must be asked to get off the bus for good. Of course, if a worker is downright nasty, open the emergency exit and boot him or her off immediately! Teamwork, consistency, and customer-driven attitudes create profits...as well as repeat business.

The incentives for excellence are powerful motivators toward better behavior. When you train people to solve problems, you must include incentives in order to cause maximum change and continuity of performance. Problem solving means that each member of your sales force or customer contact team has the authority and responsibility to create an extreme service environment on his or her own.

Banking on frustration

I needed to make a withdrawal for my 15-year-old daughter. The savings account was in her name, but it was clear that she was a minor. When I arrived with her signature on the withdrawal slip, I was told that she must appear in person to take the $60 from the account. When I objected, a control-freak teller informed me that there was no option—the bank policy dictated that the customer, even a minor, be present for a withdrawal. I asked for a manager and was told that she was, in fact, the manager and that each teller had the authority to make policy decisions. When I explained that I was a known customer to the branch and that if I had to leave and return with my daughter, the bank would be closed. No options were offered and no person could be brought to solve my problem. The absurdity of the situation gave rise to other problem—for both the bank and for me. First, I withdrew from my relationship with the bank. Secondly, I now had to travel a bit further for my banking needs. So, I sacrificed convenience for principle, and we both lost.

This is not an unusual scenario. The idea that the customer should be accommodated, regardless of silly policies, is completely foreign to someone who is not taught in creative problem solving. If each teller simply reads the manual given to him or her by the bank, the manual only dictates—it doesn't permit relationship-creating scenarios. This is part of the reason why corporate cynicism reigns and banking institutions seem to have stopped caring about the customer. Convenience and interest rate programs are the only propositions they feel the customer cares about.

There are innovators out there who defy this type of idiocy. A small bank just began a policy that is worth touting here and now:

- Open from 8 a.m. to 7 p.m., Monday through Saturday.
- Open Sunday from 10 a.m. to 4 p.m.
- 24 Hour ATM Banking (no fee regardless of the card).
- Free coffee and refreshments every minute they're open.
- Walking tellers who work the line when one exists in order to expedite transactions.
- Free checking with no minimum balance required.
- Competitive interest on all savings plans.

Extreme customer service simply began for this bank by looking at all the competition around them. They crafted a customer-driven program, recognizing that the other banks had inconvenient hours for dual income adults, mercenary policies regarding ATMs, long lines in roped-off cattle canals, checking accounts that required a minimum balance of $1,000 for free checking services, and an overall demeanor that was clearly not designed to make the customer feel welcome—much less nurtured.

What is it about a bank that should be austere? Aren't we all customers? Don't we deserve to be treated incredibly well? After all, we're leaving them with our most commercially valuable asset—our money. Why do banking personnel look so serious? Aren't they in the *ultimate* service business? The way we are treated is not only insane—but even reprehensible!

What's the solution? Reinvention! Banks need to recognize that they are only in the business to make us feel secure, well treated, happy, content, cared for, and on and on. Wouldn't it behoove the banking organization to train tellers in creating customers, rather than simply processing transactions? Transactions don't make them money, customers do.

Watch the continuing emergence of entrepreneurial, spirited enterprises in every area of commerce. High-tech is great, but high-*minded* companies are getting back to the core of business success—loving customers!

What's the customer worth?

The competition is heating up. There are more options available to the customer everyday. The creativity of younger minds is aggressively gaining ground. So, what do you do? Rest on your laurels? Perhaps...if you're independently wealthy. For example, consider that a Domino's Pizza customer is worth in excess of $7,000 in sales over a decade. The franchise owner, then has an opportunity to make approximately $700 per year from each customer who remains loyal to the franchise. If you owned a franchise, would you impart the importance of each customer to each employee? Of course you would!

Stu Leonard found out the hard way what a customer is worth to his supermarket. An innovative retailer, Leonard was approached by a longtime customer who had purchased a carton of milk and was returning it because, to her, it smelled sour. Instead of simply telling her to get another container, Leonard put the milk to his nose and violated the sacred customer credo...no believing your own customer. As soon as he placed the carton under his nose, the loyal customer became an ex-customer and Leonard lost an estimated $8,000 just from that one customer. In addition, she influenced several other customers...a potential loss of tens of thousands of dollars for the price of a quart of milk.

In Jill Griffin's book, *Customer Loyalty*, she shows that Ford Motor Company discovered that the lifetime value of a single customer represents approximately $142,000. Ford understands how critical it is to communicate with the customer on a regular basis...and trains employees at all levels and in all job descriptions that they are all customer service specialists who must recognize that their own future is tied to how well nurtured the customer feels. Further, the company recognizes that the completion of a sale is only the beginning of the profit picture.

Closing the sale and opening the relationship

"Friendship is the inexpressible comfort of having neither to weigh thoughts nor measure words" —Anonymous

In the *Guinness Book of World Records*, you'll find that the world's greatest salesman is Joe Girrard. In fact, he has the noted distinction of being the world's greatest salesman for 11 years. This guy's sold more new cars and trucks than anyone else. According to Joe, "I look at a customer as a long-term investment. I'm not just going to sell him one car. I expect to sell him every car he is ever going to buy. And, I want to sell his friends and his relatives. And when the time comes, I want to sell his children their cars too. So when somebody buys from me, he or she is going to remember me and talk about it to everybody he runs into who needs a car. I look at every customer as if they are going to be like an annuity to me for the rest of my life." In truth, what Joe Girrard does that nobody else does as well is to recognize that the close of the sale is the opening of the relationship. He stays in the customer's life with birthday greetings, anniversary cards, reminders, personal notes, updates...every conceivable reason to remain in touch is utilized to secure the relationship. It's human nature that a well- nurtured, well-loved customer will remain loyal. Extreme customer service begins when the sale is closed because that's just when the customer expects the service to stop.

Howard Zenker runs a two-store retail jewelry operation in the suburbs of Philadelphia. Howard's store has operated since the late 1800s and his father ran the business before Howard. At fifty years of age, Howard is selling engagement rings to the grandchildren of his father's customers and the children of his customers. Three generations of customers have maintained a relationship with Howard. Why? To begin with, he has what they want in the way of integrity, outstanding product design and selection, compelling quality, and competitive pricing. But, Howard has something else they want...a friend in the jewelry business. Howard's slogan (position statement) is simply "Jewelers for generations." In fact, Howard now has a relationship with grandparents, parents, children...and soon the children of the children. As young couples purchase their engagement and wedding jewelry from Howard, they go on and become parents to children—who as they grow are already following their parents' brand decision...to shop nowhere else but at Howard's store. Leaving a brand is a difficult decision for most customers. Good reasons must be in place for a customer to desert a relationship...and the reason most customers leave is indifference on the part of the business toward them. Howard recognizes that the relationship really takes hold after the sale. If that relationship flourishes, the customer's worth to the business is pronounced.

Chapter 3

Reach Them Where They Live: The Magic of the Database

If we understand the premise of *staying in touch* with the customer as a means of *keeping* the customer, how do we do it? For an answer, let's take a look at Garmany, a very prestigious men's clothing store in suburban locations outside of New York City. The first time I shopped at Garmany, I went in because they were having a sale on Hugo Boss shirts, a brand I like because of the way it fits my frame. My incentive was a 20-percent off sale, but what took place was a fine example of the kind of relationship that can only be cultivated by a dedicated system of customer connection.

The salesperson who greeted me asked if he could help me select a shirt. I was happy to have another opinion on the color. After choosing a shirt, he helped me select a few other items that caught my eye that were also on sale. When he was done, he handed me his business card and suggested that if I had any questions, or if I would like to set up an appointment for future shopping he would be delighted to assist me. He also asked if I would be willing to allow him to ask a few questions regarding my lifestyle so that when future sales occurred he would contact me in advance. The questions were simple and few. So of course I gave my name, address, phone, cloth preferences, color preferences, style preferences, and occupation.

From that point forward, I was in Garmany's database system. This system was designed to keep me as a customer through simple contact. Eventually, a card arrived in the mail in an invitation size envelope. I opened it immediately and read it. Two weeks after my initial visit, Simon, my salesperson, wrote me a note in telling me how much he appreciated my business and that he looked forward to seeing me again. Simon had simply stayed in touch, without being aggressive or obtrusive. A month later, a birthday gift arrived in a beautifully wrapped package. It was a beautiful little address book with a card from Simon. Three weeks later he jotted off a note indicating that new styles of Hugo Boss shirts arrived and would be on sale in another month. All of this attention from the purchase of one shirt and some undershorts...both of which I bought at a reduced price.

Simon had begun a relationship with me. He didn't bother me. He didn't hassle me. He didn't pursue me. He simply let me know that he cared enough about my business to stay in touch. How did I feel? I felt great and I also felt that I would shop at Garmany for my clothing needs...with Simon making the sale.

And when I shopped for a car, Richard Zambrano of Ray Catena Infiniti (one of the nation's largest dealerships) was the first person I met as I entered the showroom. However, before he discussed any automobile with me, he lead me to the back of the luxurious showroom to a cup of freshly brewed coffee. Then, as we headed to his desk, he made small talk with me. What I didn't recognize at the time was that he was finding out as much as he could about me in order to make me more comfortable and make him more able to sell me a car.

We eventually sat down and he asked what automobile I had in mind...and why. I told him that I was interested in the four wheel drive Infiniti QX4 because I liked the way it looked and my brother had ridden in one in the New Mexican desert. I even told him the color my brother had described to me. He asked me why I wanted a truck. We both agreed that it was the type of vehicle that I really needed because it made sense with the issues he brought up, such as mileage, handling, and so forth. Then, we went for a ride.

After I test drove the vehicle, we both sat and chatted again. I asked him for a price. He replied, "What would you like to pay per month on your lease?" I gave him my figures and he carefully walked me through the prices for both purchasing and leasing. I didn't tell him that I had shopped the prices with *Consumer Reports* magazine, as well as with another dealer. However, what he didn't tell me was that he knew I had done that before entering his arena. How did he know? Well, 90 percent of the automobile shoppers who come into a showroom have also shopped for prices on the Internet. Others got a price through a consumer organization. He was ready to make a sale and was not going to allow his price to be an obstacle. When he suggested a deal, it was better than the prices I had researched. I knew he had done his homework. But, I'm the type of person who does not make a high ticket purchase decision quickly, so I did what most people do...I told him that I would have to think about it, discuss it with my wife, and my business partner. Before I could finish, he threw a set of keys on the desk and said, "Don't worry about thinking about it...or anyone else's opinion." At this point I was bristling because I felt the high pressure tactics about to kick in. Before I could react or vocalize my fear, he continued, "Just take the one that's out there home for a couple of days, drive it, take the family out for a ride, show it to your business associate, and if you decide against it, I'll have somebody drive me to your home or office and I'll pick it up...no problem at all." Rich followed me in the QX4 as I drove the car home. He left the QX4 in my driveway. Within minutes, an associate from the dealership arrived to take him back. Further, he indicated that while I would always be given a loaner if I decided to make the deal, he would be happy to pick up the vehicle and deliver it back when it needed service. In addition, the two months left on my existing lease would be paid for by Ray Catena Infiniti if I wanted to sign the lease soon.

That was just the beginning. Database marketing then kicked in and a beautiful plant arrived a week following the lease. Rich sent a thank you card. A birthday card arrived soon after, then an anniversary, and a tin of cookies. I continued to arrive at the Infiniti dealer for my next car.

Ladies and gentlemen serving ladies and gentlemen

You arrive at a Ritz Carlton hotel. The bellman takes your bags and asks for your name. He asks if you've stayed at the hotel before.

When you both arrive at the front desk, the bellman asks the clerk, "Would you kindly help Mr. Jones register." The clerk states without missing a beat, "it's so good to see you again, Mr. Jones, it's been a little while, hasn't it, sir?" You respond by discussing your last visit to the area and the hotel, wondering all the while how the front desk person knew you had visited them before, without checking the computer.

What did happen? Magic? Telepathy? A great memory on the part of the hotel personnel? A certain kind of magic did take place—the magic of extreme customer service. It worked its wonders on Mr. Jones, and all the other guests who frequent the hotel. Here's how it works. The bellman asks the guest if they've stayed at the hotel before. Upon acknowledgment that the guest has visited before, he also gets a sense of the last visit. During the brief walk from the front door to the front desk the desk clerk keeps an eye on the bellman. The bellman tugs on his left ear if the guest acknowledged that he or she was a repeat guest. If the guest indicates that this is the first stay at the hotel, the bellman tugs on his right ear, in which case, the clerk handles the conversation differently. In either case, there is a keen sense that the hotel will go to great lengths to "recognize" the guest in a way that is personal, and compared to other experiences, extreme.

The mission statement of the Ritz Carlton organization is "ladies and gentlemen, serving ladies and gentlemen." Need they say more? The statement defines their reason for being as well as their purpose in the hospitality industry. It also signals who they are relative to the competition. This is called "positioning" and the Ritz Carlton has positioned themselves as more genteel than most. Of course, you pay for the privilege of being recognized and for some, it's well worth the price. For many, a clean room and comfortable bed at a low price are what's required for budget and sensibility. Clearly, the Ritz Carlton has distinguished itself by its behavior...and for those who are willing and able to pay the price, the rewards are evident.

State your position!

The position that a business assumes is extremely important to its success. Not only does your position in the marketplace define you...it defines the customer. I spoke about "hiring" the right customers and "firing" the wrong ones in my last book, *Start Up Marketing*. This issue is worth repeating and expanding upon.

When you identify the customer's needs, you begin to create a link between the business and the customer. Customers need to know what to expect from a business. By giving them what they expect (and what they *don't* expect), you exceed their need. This creates lasting impressions that will cause repeat business. From a customer service standpoint, hiring the right customers does several positive things for your business as well. It allows you to study and investigate the lifestyle needs of your "perfect" customer. When you create a customer profile, you begin a process that defines your business by defining the needs of the customer. One exacting method of creating a credible customer profile is to survey customers in a nonimposing way. By asking your customers what they want and assessing what they need, you can raise or lower your sights to accommodate them. What we want is to create as many proprietary customer service issues as possible...along with the general "treat them well" philosophy.

However, surveys are tricky and you don't want to be invasive. People will answer certain questions and ignore others, depending upon their own comfort level. For example, many customers will not reveal specific information pertaining to age, type of home, income, and other questions that may embarrass them. Our purpose in creating surveys is to fine-tune the methods we use in our customer service programs, utilizing the information appropriately. Not all customers want to be greeted in the same manner or treated the same way. Your customer is unique for a variety of reasons. You need to find out what makes each unique so that you can over-service them in areas that are most important.

The survey is a tool that may be used in person or by electronic or mail communication. The easiest method of obtaining information is to ask the customers who come in to your business to fill out a questionnaire so that you may better serve them (and to receive special incentives, promotions, and pricing). By offering an incentive, you are creating an atmosphere of exclusivity and you are implying that they are special to your business. Many companies add an immediate gratification offer to the survey in order to gain more accurate data. This is an extremely valuable method of increasing the response to your survey. Department stores do it in order to get customers to fill out a credit application for a

Our goal is to delight you!

To that end, kindly answer the following questions in order for us to include you in our database of Preferred Customers. You will receive special promotions, incentives, mailings, and pricing on future promotions. And, for taking the few moments to complete this survey, the nylon overnight bag is yours as our gift. Thank you!

1. Your name: ______________________________

2. Home address: ______________________________

____

____

3. Phone # (_____)_______-_______________

4. E-mail address: ______________________________

5. How often do you do business with us? ____________________

6. When was the last purchase made? ________________________

7. Were you treated well? (If no, please explain on back.) __________

8. How far did you travel? __________________________________

9. Please circle your household income range:

($20-$40k) ($40-$75k) (Over $75k)

10. Do you own your home or rent?

11. How many people are in your household? Adults ____Children_____

9. Do you feel your experience with us gave you good value?

Your comments please: ____

____

____

(YOUR COMPANY NAME)

We want your business today and tomorrow...and we'll do what it takes to keep you coming back!

store credit card. As soon as the information is handed to a customer service person, the customer is offered a choice of simple premiums—a water bottle, sunglasses, a velcro wallet, etc. This incentive creates responsibility on the part of the customer toward the business and, in turn, creates responses that are more valuable. A good example of a simple survey format is featured on the previous page.

The generic survey on the previous page gives you the start of a good database program that will enable you to fine-tune your customer service efforts. What we want is for the customer to allow us cater to him or her in ways that are meaningful. The purpose is to let the customer know that we care about them as individuals and want to treat them as individuals.

Customers want to be treated well. And they want to be acknowledged as having wants and needs that are specific to them. The statement following the name of the business is designed to remind the customer that this information will be utilized to make them happier and to create a business relationship that considers their feelings. The very fact that you're doing a survey communicates concern for the customer. When was the last time an airline asked you for your feelings?

Business insanity: example number 3

I visited The Home Depot recently. The chain began as a customer-driven company, grown by the boom in home sales and the economy. Indeed, it was a category buster by virtue of its size as well as the perception that the customer will be getting great service and a nice, homey experience. I bought in to the concept immediately. Being a neophyte in home improvements, I was ready to "ask the experts" for help. However, there was only one problem: There were no experts there.

I needed blacktop sealer, as well as the appropriate tools for applying this wretched goop to my driveway. I asked a salesperson I encountered and he pointed his finger into the nether areas and said, "Aisle three, I think." When we eventually found it, I told him that I had a bad back and couldn't lift the large buckets by myself. He responded by telling me to get someone in that department that *might* be able to help. Insanity? Absolutely. They slapped me in the face...after spending millions to create the impression that brought me to their business. Expectations are critical in business. If you're going to create expectations, you must meet or exceed them when the customer actually takes advantage of your product or service.

A survey gives you the ammunition you need to exceed their needs. If Home Depot cared enough about their customers, they would have surveyed me. And, perhaps they would have salvaged a customer worth saving. At this point, they've lost me forever. However, they didn't lose just me. I have a big mouth and I care about being treated well..and I'll tell others about my experiences.

Remember, surveys are optional. Customers who do not fill our surveys, in spite of incentives, are just as valuable as those who do. The idea is to be nonimposing...but creative. Creativity comes into play when you utilize the data to over-please the customer. Customers don't mind being catered to...they just don't want to be taken advantage of. Here's what I mean by a true follow-up.

Quick Chek Food Stores do customer surveys and focus studies to determine what the customer deems most important when looking for food, snacks, drinks, convenience items, or services. So, the customer is questioned and given incentives for responding. The data is then used to direct the marketing messages, the customer service issues, product development and advertising. The goal is to direct the business toward the customer's desires—not the goals of the corporation. Follow-up is done with mailings that offer the customer what they say they wanted and needed from the company. In-store surveys, telephone inquiries, and targeted promotions all maintain the intimacy with the customer so that the customer truly feels as though they've been listened to.

Turning idiosyncracy into synergy

In his book, *Customer Intimacy*, Fred Wiersema speaks of the issue of personalizing service in order to reach the individual customer. Wiersema points out that Cable & Wireless Communications, a giant in telecommunications to businesses, conducted a major survey that revealed the level of difficulty the company would have in competing with the megagiants (AT&T, MCI, and Sprint) on price. The survey indicated that customers would trade the lowest price for service options and attention that was not available at the other companies. Thus, the company used the collected data to identify a means of competing with the majors. The information revealed a desire on the part of the customer for highly customized, feature-laden phone services that would provide value added benefits to the small and midmarket companies (a huge portion of the market).

Then, CWI divided its 48 sales offices in the United States to operate as separate companies. More than just a philosophical approach to problem solving, they actually empowered each office to find specific solutions to each customer in that market. As separate companies, the offices needed to pay particular attention to the differences and subtleties in each community. Each of these separate companies took responsibility for their own group of customers and thus began an evolutionary change in the way they compete and do business.

What they discovered through customer surveying is that there are more valuable components to the business relationship than price alone. According to CWI's president and CEO, Gabriel Battista, "the long-distance market is less and less about price and more about service." Battista strongly feels that segmentation and total customer responsiveness will triumph in his industry. This feeling is not based upon opinion...it is based upon a radical concept: *Asking the customer what is most important*!

The idea of niche marketing for reasons of understanding the customer's needs and wants is actually quite profound. When we divide our database into similar customers and similar responses, we can create a targeted approach to nurture the customer in specific ways. The database/survey system of creating extreme customer service programs is hard work, but it's the finest method of achieving breakthrough results in furthering a business's agenda.

Chapter 4

Welcome to the Land of Big

The big dog. The biggest sandwich this side of the Pecos. The big kahuna. The biggest store. The supermarket. The giant burger. The giant waterslide. The tallest man. Skyscrapers. Megamergers. Jumbo jets. Super Subs. The incredible Hulk. Mount Everest. The Washington Monument. The World Trade Center. The Empire State Building. The Sears Tower. The largest ball of twine in the world. The largest nonstick frying pan. The longest stretch limo. The largest cruise ship.

Got it? I hope so. The list is endless. We live in the land of big. Bigger is better. Bigger is best. Bigger is, well, bigger. If you travel through the country you'll see an abundance of giant things. The concept doesn't communicate value, quality, taste, or even comparable size...it just says **bigger is better!** We all know the adage that size doesn't count...or does it? The truth is that customers can, on some levels, relate to the issue of big as a selling proposition. But what is big? Is it necessarily better?

What benefit can the customer perceive as valuable to him or her from a message about size? What is the perceived value to the customer? The answer is that big is a cultural icon in and of itself. If we can turn the idea of *big* into *better*, then bigger *is* truly better and the customer will see the benefits of the size/value relationship.

Recently, I consulted with a client that sells sub sandwiches in a highly competitive East Coast metropolitan market. The issue of quality has long been dealt with in a variety of ways. The company pays particular attention to utilizing the finest provisions, the freshest produce, the highest quality baked goods—all in an ongoing effort to outlcass the competition. But, in an increasingly competitive market, the concept of quality alone was tougher to constantly communicate. It was a message that had probably reached its peak within the context of the marketplace. People got it...and sales reflected it. However, the next step was to invent an issue that provided more to the customer than the competition. Remember, in designing a customer driven company, we constantly look to the competition for gaping holes, vacuums, and voids. Here's where size entered the arena. My client owned quality and was keenly competitive on price. What we decided was that, with a minor modification to the product, we could create a sub that was two inches longer and slightly heavier than the competitive products. Remember, we already owned the important issues...now we were going after size. By announcing that the standard sub was eight inches instead of six and had more meat, cheese, and fixings, we created an entirely new product and an entirely new selling proposition. The company communicated its goal to constantly over-please the patron.

We knew we were better... now we need to be bigger!

By using size to sell, value and customer concern became tangible assets. What was communicated in a variety of ways was "You deserve a better sub...we're just giving you more of it—an extra three bites on us!"

Bigger can definitely be better when it produces a customer benefit that outperforms any other product in the market. This client doesn't rely upon subjective judgments alone to assess the value of an idea. Each issue is surveyed, studied, and analyzed in order to ensure that the customer's desires are paramount. Customer-driven companies are run by the customers...not top management.

Watch out, bigger can backfire!

Look at some of the biggest names in business. IBM, Coca-Cola, AT&T, General Motors, Microsoft, Apple, McDonald's, The United States government, etc. Fred Wiersema, author of *Customer Intimacy*, points out that bigger can bust. The idea that giants are looking out for the customer is one that needs to be reexamined. Companies need to understand what big is and what big does.

Wiersema discussed what had gone wrong at IBM. The answer he obtained came from a former president of one of IBM's country operations. He told Wiersema that, "the company had lost its soul." Apparently, for decades IBM had navigated from a three-point credo established by its long-time boss, Thomas Watson. Watson's philosophy was based upon the notion that you must respect the individual, look after the customer's well-being, and go the extra distance to assure the best results. But the company's commitment to those principles had weakened. The result was the decline of the most famous and successful customer-intimate corporation in history.

Wiersema points out that to an outsider, Watson's credo might sound like commercial piety. But to those inside IBM, it encapsulated what the company and employees of IBM stood for.

John Foster, Chairman of NovaCare, points out, "I ask myself why it is that so many of the companies I've worked for don't exist anymore, when other organizations like the Girl Scouts or the Bolshoi Ballet or the Marine Corps go on and on? My answer is that the other organizations stand for something."

Wiersema is quick to point out an example of this critical issue which separates big from good. Northwestern Mutual Life Insurance Company has a position statement that defines its reason for being better, not bigger. "We exist for the benefit of our policyholders." President and CEO Jim Ericson declares: "What it says is that we are the policy holders' company. That's what mutual means—that we are owned by our customers. Everything we do—every decision we make is based on what we think is good for our customers and our owners. It gives us a unique culture."

We're not in business to please ourselves. We're not in business to create extreme service issues that benefit our bottom line without first benefitting the needs and desires of the customer. We're in business to excite and delight the customer in significant, tangible ways...a theme I'll repeat throughout this book.

Many big companies have lost their way. Recently, I was asked during a TV interview what had gone wrong with Apple before they reclaimed their market presense. I was blindsided because the interview was about small businesses, entrepreneurial businesses...and I wasn't prepared to delve into the many facets of Apple. I quickly responded with a statement that I believe applies to so many giants who have forgotten their reason for being in business. Apple began believing its own success and forgot about the customer. Apple underestimated the marketplace and was left with a selling proposition that had become dated and dull. As we evolve in business, becoming bigger is often the biggest problem we have...because it affords us the false sense of security that permits us to cloud our thinking and fuzzy up our judgment.

Coca-Cola looked at a myriad of options when it decided to bring out a new product. What it didn't take into account was that the customer didn't want or need a new product. Customer-driven companies are run by the customer, not the upper management. Coca-Cola forgot that you don't allow that to happen to your business. Extreme customer service exists to create golden opportunities between you and the customer, based upon the customer's desires. If you ask, they will come. If you listen, they will act.

Banking on your trust

In *Tales of Knock Your Socks Off Service,* authors Kristin Anderson and Ron Zemke point out some inspiring big stories. For example, they tell the tale of Norwest Bank, a bank with 800 branches in 16 states with 53,000 employees and $80 billion in assets. The employees are steeped in a culture of customer service and are passionate about retail banking, which according to *The Wall Street Journal*, makes Norwest pretty unusual.

"Most bankers consider retail branches so expensive that they should be replaced by automated teller machines and 'home banking,'" *The Wall Street Journal* writes. "Personal service, they believe, must be reserved for the affluent. Norwest Corporation has another idea. It actually encourages visits by the less-than-affluent, offering free coffee and cookies to senior citizens the day Social Security checks are issued" (*WSJ*, August 17, 1995).

I have a client who would refer to the less-than-affluent senior citizens as "flies." Why? Because according to this retailer, "they come in, buzz around, eat the candy, and buy nothing." I disagree. The "flies" as he refers to them are the foundation of many businesses...because they are loyal and communicate their business relationships to anyone who will listen. They've got lots of time on their hands and not a lot of distractions, and they need community businesses to recognize them with a friendly environment and a cup of coffee.

Richard Kovacevich, CEO of Norwest Bank, recognizes that long term success does not exclusively rest on community based banking or 'smart' cards. Nor does he believe in charging customers for the privilege of talking to a teller (like Fleet Bank and others do). He doesn't believe in forcing customers to use an ATM so he can cut labor costs. He believes the bank's success now, and in the future, depends upon having the products customers need and want and providing service that makes them comfortable and happy that they've chosen *his* bank. What does great service look like? According to *Tales of Knock Your Socks Off Service*, it looks like this:

In Mesa, Arizona, Tim Huish received a phone call from a man who needed a document notarized—the man, a double amputee, had called Huish's branch of Norwest in desperation. He was a customer of a different bank and had just been told that he'd have to bring the document to the bank to have it notarized because the bank didn't make house calls. Huish and Theresa Holmes, another Mesa Norwest employee, drove to the man's home, did the notarization, and ensured that the man's documents were headed off to their proper destination. Any guesses where the man decided to move his bank accounts to?

Bigger can be better, obviously, by the example shown at Norwest. But why wouldn't most companies prefer a posture of extreme service to one of indifference? Because sometimes bigger means that companies begin to believe their own success. IBM believed their own press. Apple bought into its own superstar status. Coca-Cola believed it could do no wrong. The entire airline industry continues to act as though their monopoly on long distance travel permits them to mistreat the public.

But why, if treating customers well and earning their respect—possibly even their love—would create profits, wouldn't everyone make it part of their agenda? Sure it costs some time and money...but so does trying to put out fires.

Barry Williams is a 32-year-old millionaire working for a Wall Street brokerage firm. Barry targets companies doing between five and fifty million dollars. He considers himself a midmarket specialist in investment instruments, retirement funds, and stock and bond trading. Barry has created a very personal approach to his business. He offers to review a company's retirement programs at no cost or obligation. He also issues a report by e-mail, fax, or courier, so that his selling is first done totally by the numbers. If he can prove that his recommended portfolio would have outperformed the company's existing one, he simply asks for a meeting. He's been very successful.

However, he does something else, too. He communicates with each employee at his own expense (once given the approval to do so) in order to establish a meeting when everyone can attend. The meeting can be held at his office (where he serves light fare) in order to present the program and illustrate the comparisons. Furthermore, he establishes one nonnegotiable ground rule. The decision to choose him cannot be made for one month from the presentation in order for each employee to track certain investments that he presents to them! If, in that one month's time, the recommended investments have not outperformed their existing portfolio, he asks for one more month and then leaves the prospects to their own decisions. He simply puts his expertise on the line by taking all the responsibility and permits everyone to see the enormous size of his company—even though they represent smaller than usual clients. This does several things. First, the size of the company would be typically too intimidating for the audience. This presentation permits them to feel accommodated by such a giant Wall Street firm. Secondly, it allows each participant to see that the size has a distinct advantage when it comes to research, services, experience, and commitment. Next, it puts smaller businesses in an environment with large businesses and allows aspirations to fly.

When companies use their size to a positive advantage, size does matter. According to Anderson and Zemke, The Norwest Nth Degree ethic works because it is a top-to-bottom ethic. The example they give illustrates how a customer discovered that she had arrived just a bit too late at a branch office in Arizona. Apparently, the woman was desperate and needed a cashier's check to close the escrow for a new home. A stranger on the street asked her why she looked so saddened and she related the story of arriving at the bank after business hours. He rather brazenly knocked on the glass door, catching the attention of a teller. He motioned the teller to come to the door, whereupon the teller opened the door, wrote the check, acknowledged the customer's need...and the rest is history.

Only later did she learn that the mysterious stranger on the street was Jon Campbell, president and CEO of Norwest Bank, Arizona, who happened to be leaving the bank. It's a big bank with rules, services, employees, time tables, and computers that need to be shut down at the end of each day. But big clearly means "big minded" in the case of Norwest. The sad fact is that these examples are few and far between.

Super marketing

Did you ever wander into a supermarket and find a product that is a small brand, or perhaps even an unknown brand. Most of us aspire to big brands because we tend to trust big. However, marketers recognized that many little companies were catching the attention of the customer, just because they weren't big. Because they are smaller, a customer feels the company is more service-driven and clearly more community-minded.

When Hallmark (the giant card company) decided that the little card companies were chipping away at their global empire, they gobbled many of them along the way. However, they then decided to start their own "little" company in order to compete with themselves. So Shoebox Greeting Cards was established as a "tiny little division of Hallmark." This niche branding was done because the perception is that extreme service behavior is more apt to come from a smaller, more intimate company...indeed, a less commercial personality.

In his *Circle of Innovation*, Tom Peters refers to "The Age Of Narrowcasting" or "One-to-one marketing." According to this philosophy, each and every customer would become a market and the company would cater to that customer with customized services and products. For some enterprises this is a novel idea. However, for most businesses, the preferred method of marketing extreme customer service is to customize en masse. Mass customization, like Land's End is a perfect example of mass marketing with a distinct twist toward the individual. The sophistication of their database management permits them to appear intimate by starting a conversation with the customer. From the information the company retrieves through surveys and past orders, a profile of the customer is used and the company can communicate in a more intimate fashion. According to Tom Peters, mass customization is a real goal of many companies of global proportion such as Nike, Rubbermaid, Snapple, Saturn, Virgin Atlantic, MTV, MCI, CNN, and so on.

If you're so big, why aren't you generous?

In a recent *New York Times* article, "You Buy It, You Keep It, More Stores Are Saying," Monique Yazigi points out some stunning stories about big companies with small-minded thinking.

Virginia Sullivan was walking up Park Avenue trying to keep all her packages balanced. She is the epitome of the hardened New York shopper but she readily admitted to the *New York Times* reporter that she no longer can tolerate the exhausting chore of attempting to return unsatisfactory merchandise. She related, "anytime I've tried to return something, people in the store make me feel embarrassed, dishonest—almost like I'm a criminal."

She related that she has a closet full of clothing with tags attached to prove it. The conclusion: It's easier to buy than to return!

Retail analysts looked at megagiants in the industry, as well as smaller boutiques. They found that return policies have become much leaner and much meaner than ever before. Regardless of size, companies were turning their backs on consumers...with complaints ranging from cold salespeople who seem to have been trained to intimidate customers out of returning merchandise, to ridiculously short return periods and store credits instead of refunds. Where has civility gone?

The article further states the experience of a customer attempting to return a Prada bag after more than 10 days. If the model is no longer in stock, there's no return. At Daffy's, an off-price, creative retailer in the metropolitan area, if the price ticket is not attached, there's no return. What about gifts?

L.L. Bean was once known for taking back 30-year-old Hudson's Bay point blankets, no questions asked. They have become more restrictive in their returns as well. According to, Rich Donaldson, a spokesman for L.L. Bean, "the policies started tightening up two years ago. We now ask customers for the reasons they are dissatisfied." The company's policy is meant to discourage the kind of shopper who showed up at the flagship store in Freeport, Maine, last year and he tried to trade in a pair of worn-out Bluchers. The sales associate looked dismayed and simply asked the customer why not throw them away?

Analysts suggest that, as competition heats up in the retail arena, customer service suffers...a sad fact when you consider that it was the reason many retail organizations became prominent. Astonishingly, there have been no surveys of customer attitudes toward return policies, interviews with shoppers on the finest shopping streets in New York City revealed many tales of shopping misery. The legendary giants in the department store industry have begun to follow the suit established by the restrictive smaller boutiques and it's leaving customers in the dust. The article pointed out a stunning example of the mean spirit in retailing today. A woman shopped in Robert Clergerie shop on Madison Avenue in Manhattan. She brought back a pair of shoes, pointing out that the heel had broken on one of them. The salesman dismissed her with a curt, "Sorry, we have no responsibility for that," the woman said.

When asked about the incident, Kim Gracianette, the store's manager, said that Robert Clergerie's return policy hadn't changed in recent years, and that the New York branches of the French chain were more lenient than their foreign counterparts. In France they say, "we're not Maytag—you buy it, it's yours." The only allowance they will make is credit on credit cards if the merchandise is returned with a receipt within 10 days of purchase.

Customers can ruin it for other customers

Are there customers who ruin return policies? Absolutely! The boorish behavior of a small segment of the population can topple some mighty generous and creative examples of customer service, and it's a shame. The fact is, there is a portion of the population who will purchase a winter coat for a week long vacation in the northeast...only to return it before they head back to their homes in Florida. It does happen and it's hideous. But, for the most part, the abuses are minor and the reaction more major.

Even the Gap, known for its generous rules, is clamping down. The chain recently reduced its period for price adjustment—the time during which a customer who buys an item at full retail price may claim a rebate if the item later goes on sale. Now, the customer must return the item with its receipt within 14 days, instead of 30, as before, and may do so only once, rather than two or three times, as some once did.

According to Bruce Van Kleeck, a vice-president of the National Retail Federation, "Unfortunately, a number of consumers began to take advantage, returning items that would not normally be returned. Returns are expensive items." The truth is that retailers feel as though they're fighting back to protect themselves from dishonest customers...a clear example of a few apples spoiling the whole bunch! The truth is, extreme customer service cannot exist without the acknowledgment that abuses can go both ways. We have to be reasonable in our expectations and reasonable in our behavior toward the businesses we encounter.

Many large corporations are, in fact, turning to consultants for help in solving this dilemma. The Service Quality Institute is a 25-year-old organization and the global leader in helping organizations keep customers, build market share, and improve the performance of their work force to deliver superior customer service. (You can visit them on the Internet at www.customer-service.com/mainf.html)

The president and founder of the Service Quality Institute is John Tschohl, *Time and Entrepreneur* magazine's "Customer Service Guru." He has established offices of the Institute around the world. They offer a free newsletter for organizations both large and small. I listed their Web address above, and they can be reached at:

Service Quality Institute
9201 East Bloomington Freeway,
Minneapolis, MN 55420-3437
Phone: (612) 884-3311; Fax: (612) 884-8901
E-Mail: quality@servicequality.com

The Institute's consulting services are worthy of a review—whether your company is starting out in manufacturing, distribution, technology, retailing, or direct mail. The services include a host of issues that are truly compelling and can help focus a small company on philosophies that can help it evolve into a big company.

So, in the final analysis, is bigger better? The answer is that it's always better to be better first and bigger second. When both become part of your culture, the bottom line is larger profits, repeat business, and loyal customers.

Chapter 5

Civility and Common Sense

"Learn to use the "W" word (wow) and the "L" word (lust)...or perish!"
—Tom Peters, *The Circle of Innovation*

You've all heard the tired, drab, horribly-cliched phrases about customer service: "Satisfy the customer," or "conform to requirements." According to Tom Peters, these and most other statements made by business owners are "dry" to say the least.

So, where do we begin in our quest to excite and delight...to wow the customer in ways that others can't, won't, or haven't yet? Well, we should begin at the beginning. Let's define business civility. Truly, it begins with the notion that, as civilized people, we often act uncivilly toward each other. After all, social civility is still a problem in our culture. As social creatures, we develop our skills by being taught how to behave. For most of us, this begins with our parents, teachers, friends, family members, authorities, co-workers, bosses, or customers. These background rules of behavior are what psychologists refer to as "conditioned responses." What these can mean in our businesses have to do with the development of our employees, customers, or coworkers. If the desired response is happy people, the gesture must set that situation up in tangible ways.

Many years ago, I had a client who began every conversation with me, my staff, his own team...even his own customers...by stating, "what are you trying to get away with now?"

This probably wasn't his fault. He was trained to "do it to them before they do it to you." The problem was that he had not evolved...not personally, not socially, not commercially in his behavior toward others. His premise was that everybody was out to get him—including his customers. As a giftware manufacturer, he always felt that the buyers were out to get him by negotiating return policies, slow payments...hundreds of issues that keep him from feeling good about the sales relationship. In truth, Jerry wasn't a happy man in many areas of his life. The tragic aspect of his unhappiness is that it cost him his business when his business was what took him closest to happiness.

Jerry acted like a curmudgeon and his customers became disenchanted. If we're in the professional service business, then we have a responsibility to understand that the only product we have to sell is ourselves...the only product! If we sell cars, we're selling ourselves, but we share the spotlight with the object. In the case of services, there's no other object than our honesty, integrity, and passion!

If you have ever studied the writings of the Dalai Lama, you know that this gentle leader, philosopher, and statesman has devoted his life to understanding life. According to the Dalai Lama, the goal of living is to find happiness. It's a wonderful goal and one that we don't seem to carry over to our vocations. In truth, we spend far more time in life working than in recreation...with most Americans devoting barely two weeks per year to vacation and many Americans spending eight to 12 hours per day working, 50 plus weeks per year. Why not create some happiness in the workplace for you and your customers? Why can't we begin to understand that there's nothing particularly noble about working hard when hard work doesn't equate to smart work? Jerry worked hard...he never worked smart. In the final analysis, he sold his business for half of its worth because his reputation among his customers had become so diminished by his cynicism and negativity.

If a business has no common sense, what sense is there in doing business with them?

There's a lovely barrier reef resort island near Atlantic City, New Jersey, called Long Beach Island. There are probably ten or so boat rental places on the island. They all have the same thing in common—they rent you a boat.

However, let's examine this "boat renting paradigm" for a moment. They're in the boat rental business, they have boats they rent for profit, they advertise and compete with one another for the vacationer's business, they sell supplies, refreshments, bait—and yet they will do everything possible to discourage you from a truly happy experience.

Here's the typical scenario. You read their ad about renting pontoon boats for $250 per day. You show up with your family and are told you need a reservation because there's only one pontoon boat available. Frustrated, you make a reservation for the following day and are told that you must be there promptly at 7:45 a.m. in order to get out on the water by 8:30 a.m. The list of restrictions and regulations you need to follow is substantial. Then you review where you *can* and *cannot* go. You're fitted for life vests, sold some supplies that you're told you need—only to discover that the $250 doesn't include gas. After all of this, you need to leave both a major credit card and a $200 cash deposit. The worst obsticle, barring all of the legalistic forms and hidden fees, was the proprietor's rotten attitude to me, *his customer*. Every conceivable obstacle is thrown at you before you leave the dock...to have fun.

Many businesses are founded on suspicion and skepticism. The business posture is to assume that the customer is out to get the business owner. The boat rental company owner presumably chose that type of business because of inheritance, knowledge, passion...oops, did we say passion? It didn't appear so by our treatment there. Tom Peters tells us that passion equates to success. I agree that passion is a necessary component of success and clearly a necessary part of extreme customer service.

Well, back to the boat guy. I signed the sheets, filled out the disclaimers, handed over the money, tried on the life jacket, started the engine, took the boat out and, in spite of the sour personality and the intolerable process of simply renting a boat, sailed off for a pleasurable day. Upon returning, no one asked how my day was, or how much fun we had, or where we went, or if the kids were able to catch any crabs. The transaction was completed only by virtue of contracted arrangements. Would I ever return to that shop? I'd rather strap a barrel to my back and float out to sea.

When we recognize that fun *is* the foundation of business...and that relationships are the primary reason people return to any business, we're on our way out of commodization, frustration, or failure. Let's face it, whether we're selling a product or service, we're selling ourselves in the transaction in some way, shape, or form. As Peters claims, we need to have **zero tolerance** for simple commoditization, especially in service fields.

Peters's profound claim is that the delivery of a professional service is absolutely nothing more than the delivery of the person him- or herself. After all, he points out, "When you look in the mirror at 6 a.m., is the person you see a commodity?" No, the person you see is *you* and *you* alone. Each individual brings unique characteristics to the business equation that must be exploited in creative ways. If you didn't believe this, you'd have purchased another book...perhaps one titled, *Just Say Maybe*! We are what we act!

Passion can't be learned—it must be felt. Developing social and business skills that will identify you as a brand can be learned. In a recent issue of *New York* magazine, the feature article, "Brand New You," focused on how each of us can burnish our professional image by turning ourselves into a brand. The article also went on to offer classes in self-branding.

When you focus on a business leader's persona and passion, you can invite intimacy and connection between the buyer and the seller of the comapny. This works, because your customer can feel a sense of the person behind the corporate veil. This causes the customer to relate to the individual in a far more human way.

Small, entrepreneurial businesses can now distinguish themselves as extreme examples of excellence by creating branding initiatives for products, services, and people. The marketing phrase, "top of mind," has been replaced by its new millennial counterpart, "mindshare." Mindshare refers to distinguishing marks, attributes, and talents that people think about when they think about you. Indeed, the concept of mindshare is the central element in self-branding. Mindshare tells the world who and what you are, what your potential is, and where your passion truly is. The article gives convincing examples of this concept.

For example, most people know that former Treasury Secretary Robert Rubin is an avid fly fisherman. His brand identity reflects patience, contemplation, and sagacity. Tom Brokaw has let it be known that his passion is fly fishing as well...an issue that creates a brand identity for Brokaw as reflective, even poetic and romantic.

On the brainier side, there's Microsoft's Nathan Myhrvold, who is a master chef, or Tony Bennett's persona as a painter, or Ronald Perelman's reputation as a drummer as well as a mild-mannered financier. These are the "adhesive" images that the world loves to see and acknowledge. The mindshare concept allows us to see the human side, the personal, private world of people we come in contact with through media, or through our own personal experiences. This branding notion draws us closer to the individual and the business.

From Middle C to big blue sea

Paul Santo owns Santo Marine, a beautiful marina with little boats, sailboats, big power boats, and other personal watercraft docked all along it. Santo Marine brokers boats, stores boats, and has many longstanding customers who keep their boats in his slips, using the lovely waters of the bay and the Atlantic ocean nearby. Paul Santo knows a lot about boats. He is easily distinguished as an independent cuss who cares far more about relationships than simple bottom-line business deals. In fact, he occasionally buys old wooden boats and moors them in his marina, with no intention of selling them. He does this so he can see them when he's seated at his cluttered desk in a trailer-office. Paul often can be found staring out the window near his desk—simply looking at some of his boats as though they were paintings hanging in a gallery. I asked him once if he ever uses them. "Nope," said Paul. "I just like looking at them."

However, Paul's other passion is pianos and it's evident when you visit the marina or speak to Paul. He loves pianos and (much to his wife's chagrin) collects them. Paul is so passionate about pianos, he'll often spend more time looking for them than he will for boats...but that's okay, because when you buy a boat from Paul, you're buying Paul.

Extreme customer service for Paul Santo begins by letting the customer know who and what he is, and it continues when Paul gets to know you. Immediately you sense that this is not an ordinary businessman, one who is primarily interested in closing the sale. Paul is interested in closing the relationship—not the sale itself. I actually didn't buy my boat from Paul. I ended up buying a boat from a competitor. However, we remain friends and one of my most pleasurable pastimes is stopping by to chat with Paul about boats, pianos, or just to have lunch together. The world needs more Pauls in it...people who care more about the connection than the contract.

Successful people are generally people who reach well beyond the standards of business...those who reach into the hearts of those they do business with. The guy who rents boats for a living will probably always earn a living, but he'll never earn the kind of relationships that translate a living into an empire. Paul Santo, in his own small universe, has created a world of relationships that will remain loyal to him forever, and he will grow his business to the degree he desires because he has a base of customers who will continually refer others to him.

Rules are made to be broken

I love Tom Peter's adage, "Rules are for fools." As he points out, if you play by the rules, there's no chance your name will enter the list with Stanley Marcus, Richard Branson, Wayne Huizenga, Donna Karan, and yes, Paul Santo!

Visionary behavior begins by recognizing that if you reverse the rules, you're beginning a process of innovation, a standard of creativity that will permit, invite, entice, and seduce customers into loving you as much as you love them. We need to give people more than expected, removing every conceivable obstacle that stands in the way of doing more business, communicating trust to those who line our pockets every day.

If the customer is always right, why do I usually feel wronged?

We all agree that customers are the reason businesses thrive. Can you imagine a successful business without customers? If we agree that every single business in the world depends upon the customer, then why do businesses pay so little attention to serving our needs, fulfilling the customer's desires in order to get it?

We need to put our needs on the line with the businesses we do business with. Sometimes that requires us to be more demanding in communicating what we expect as customers. Consider the fact that an irate customer, at his own expense, can run a Web site that can discredit your business. His revenge, as a highly disgruntled customer, is to post the abuses he endured from a your company. The Internet is a powerful public forum for "fighting back" against poor or abusive treatment because of its widespread use.

The idea of civility is a radical concept to many businesses and service industries—from doctors, lawyers, accountants, engineers, dentists, insurance agents, and stockbrokers—and it stems from the fact that nobody in the education of any of these professions taught civility, decency, common sense. Businesses have become cynical toward the customer. Customers have come to accept (even expect) poor service because the idea of civility is not common to our culture.

I have a buying motto which is: "What's in it for me?" It's not an aggressive posture, rather it is one which places certain demands on the relationships I have with the businesses in my life. For example, I'll ask my insurance agent to update me on the most recent legislation, changes in policies, or better premium opportunities. I demand that the communication between us is constant and value-oriented so that I can feel as though I have a personal advocate working on my behalf on all of these issues. When I shop for a car, I ask to be introduced to the manager, service manager, and the owner of the dealership. I place certain demands on the organization that raises their awareness about my expectations as a customer. It works. When we tell businesses what we expect, we're establishing some ground rules and demanding a sense of purpose and civility to the relationship. If they're really smart, they'll constantly exceed our expectations and win us over as customers forever. If they're not terribly smart, they'll simply meet our needs and expectations. If they're incredibly stupid, they'll ignore us...and we won't be ignored!

Many companies use technology to create an even broader gap between us...by making it more difficult to actually connect with a real person. Technology can enhance customer relations as well as hinder them, but, for the most part, high-tech materials have created a greater gap between customer and company.

The danger of technology is that it permits companies to ignore us with greater ease. Voice mail, e-mail, fax machines, Internet services, Web communication—all distance us from the company, and, if they so desire, they can use this distance to frustrate us into submission.

A funny thing happened on the way to the pizzeria!

My son loves one particular pizzeria in our town. There are many pizzerias, but one place has captured his attention more than others (it stemmed mostly from getting some free stickers at this place). Needless to say, I am well known to the owners.

However, on this particular occasion, I ordered four slices of pizza...and was charged the same amount as a whole pie. When I asked the owner, his response was swift and authoritative. "Your ordered four slices at two dollars per slice and that's our price per slice (what a poet). If you ordered a whole pie, the cost is eight dollars. That's our price for a whole pie." "Where's the logic?" I asked. He told me that the menu clearly stated the prices and I should read before I order. When I asked again, in a friendly tone, what sense that made, he shook is head as though he was just asked the square root of a ten digit number. "What do you want me to do?" he asked. I told him that I thought it would have been reasonable for him to point out that I could get a whole pie for the same amount...or to charge me less for just four slices. When he began to appear upset with me, I asked him a simple question. "What am I worth to you?" He looked stunned and bewildered, so I helped him along. "I spend several thousand dollars a year in your restaurant. In fact, you catered my daughter's sweet sixteen just three months ago. What am I worth as a customer to you?" He told me to take the whole pie—that he didn't have time to play games. Civility, common sense, and relationships were all foreign concepts to the man behind the counter. I figure that he lost in excess of $4,000 just by treating me with complete indifference. Then, he lost the business of everyone I encounter in relating this story.

Compromise is part of customer service. It's something we as customers can expect to do sometimes and what we can demand from businesses as well. The truth is that extreme customer service exists as an anomaly in our culture while it should be the norm. Only when we tell the receptionist at the dentist's office that we expect to be treated well do we have a chance of being treated well. The power we possess is in the increased options we have as customers. We now have more choices than ever in every service field and area of business.

So, the next time you feel not cared for, abused, or worse—treated with indifference—try asking the business owner what he or she will do for you that the other store down the street won't. In essence, you're demanding that they distinguish themselves, create a brand identity for themselves, and position their businesses in a positive way that you can relate to as a customer who expects to be delighted!

Fighting for your rights as a customer

Retailer News offers creative business solutions for those in the retail trade. In a recent edition of its newsletter, Rich Kizer and Georganne Bender related a wonderful example of the nation's foremost forward thinking retail organization: Nordstrom.

They told a story of about making a purchase at a popular store in their town. When they got home, they discovered that they were overcharged. They immediately called the store to correct the problem and were told that they would have to call back on Monday in order to remedy the situation (it was Saturday). They hastily asked to speak to the store manager. They walked through the entire story once again—in between being put on hold while being force-fed every Barry Manilow song ever written. Finally after frustrating moments of waiting and tapping their fingers to "Mandy," they straightened out the situation with the manager.

However, two days later, they walked into a Nordstrom store to exchange a defective blazer and were met with "no problem." The salesperson immediately offered a refund or a replacement blazer—their mission was accomplished. What a difference between the sensibilities of the two organizations. The training at every level was evident in Nordstrom, yet the other store never trained or empowered any employee to act responsibly, upholding the integrity of the corporate mission.

Imagine how much opportunity exists for you—considering the low levels of service in every area of business today. Self-serve environments have fostered a low level of expectation as well, so a strong service story has success written all over it. Because the surveys indicate that consumers are so disgusted today, any kind of special service is deemed exceptional. Remember, customers want help when they want it and they want to be left to their own devices when they want that. So, it's your responsibility to understand the fine line between being helpful and being annoying. It's critical to recognize that extreme customer service is a nonthreatening system, not one that annoys and hard-sells the customer.

Because most customers' first impressions of a company are formed by their encounters with employees, you have to ask yourself, what is the first impression my customers are getting when they contact my company, when they come in the door, when they inquire on the phone or on-line? An example given in the recent issue of *Retailer News* is about Patches, a country gift and collectable business in Emmaus, Pennsylvania. The owner, Pat Nolte, believes in "one-on-one training." She says, "I never leave my people alone until I am comfortable with their knowledge of the store. I start slowly, working first on customer service and product knowledge. During this training period, I am able to determine what their special talents are, and can encourage them to grow from there." Pat Nolte recognizes that anyone on the front line in her organization can either foster her growth or sabotage the business...sometimes simply by appearing ignorant about the products or indifferent toward the customers.

When it comes to training their team, Don and Jane Marski, owners of Hannah's Home Accents in Antioch, Illinois, are two very aggressive trainers. In addition to traditional training meetings, they move things out onto the sales floor once a month to allow associates to take an educational tour of the store. Associates see what's in, what's out, what's new, hot, and happening.

In order to assess your own ability to implement extreme service behavior toward the customer, you'll need a sense of your competition. Kizer and Bender suggest an exercise called, "How Did It Feel." This program begins by sending an employee to a competitor's store to look for an unfamiliar item. Tell the employee to come as close to purchasing the item as possible, without actually doing so. Have him or her ask a salesperson for help. Have the employee ask lots of questions about the item or its uses. The employee has only twenty minutes to complete this experience. Once the employee returns to your business, ask how everything went, and most importantly, how it felt to be a customer. It can be incredibly frustrating to be a customer today, and frustration is a feeling you never want your customers to have. The employee sees the other side of the experience as a customer and can incorporate the experience into his or her own job performance. After this exercise, your employee will be able to identify your competition's strengths, weaknesses, the voids that exist in the service, and the level of product knowledge on the part of the sales staff.

Rick Phillips, author of an article entitled, "Want More Ideas on How to Increase Sales and Profits? Ask Your Customers," writes about an experience he had with a business that failed to heed the notion that the customer is (at least) sometimes right. He told a story about a visit to a car dealership. The business was family owned for about a quarter of a century and had a good reputation within the community. Rick had some minor problems with his car that were not being resolved by the dealership, so he decided to talk to the sales manager in an attempt to get past the problems. After describing the issues to the sales manager, the man looked at Rick with a blank stare and said, "it sounds like a service problem. Why are you talking to me? I head up the sales department."

Frustrated, Rick explained that he was addressing this issue with him because he was in sales and he was presumably responsible for Rick's happiness as it related to the dealership. He also explained that he speaks to an average of 50 people per day and would be delighted to begin a campaign that would relate the problems to all his associates, friends, family, and acquaintances. Astonishingly the sales manager seemed unmoved.

"Mr. Phillips," responded the indignant sales manager, "I hear your kind of threats every day. To be frank with you I can't be worried about them or you." Well, both parties kept their mutual commitments and Rick spoke often about the indignities of dealing with the dealership and the sales manager remained unconcerned. It took 18 months for the dealership to file bankruptcy and liquidate the business. Rick elaborates on this issue with several points worth noting here.

First, customers will tell us about the future, if we listen carefully. If you listen to them, they'll tell you what their needs are, what their concerns are, and what their fears are. However, when we don't listen to the customer and exceed their expectations, we will fail.

Secondly, customers will give us good ideas...if we're open to them. Because customers are removed from our businesses, they have insights that we may not recognize. They approach their relationship with a particular business with the question, "why not" instead of what many business owners say to themselves, "it can't be done."

The president of Quick Chek Food Stores has a framed poster on his wall. It simply says: "If you can say it can't be done, you're right...you can't do it!" If someone cannot do their job to the extreme, they'll get someone with a better attitude to get it done.

Thirdly, customers will offer us insight and information about how we're doing what we're doing. If we truly establish a platform that invites the customer to speak—and strongly suggests that we'll listen—things will evolve for the better. I've even had the idea of a "fireside chat" where customers are invited once a quarter to an evening where they can share ideas and express their positive and negative comments to the president of the company they're doing business with. Radical? I don't think so. It's an invitation to join the community and an invitation to become part of the corporate family.

Phillips says that face-to-face listening should be an ongoing process between all customer relations people and all customers. When the waitress asks, "is everything all right", she may say it without any expectation of receiving a negative response. But a customer-driven company asks for a reason...and follows up with more engaging questions...like, "how could we have made this experience even better, do you have any thoughts?" The magic in getting customers to talk is to ask questions that require specific answers.

You need nutrition for your business, not attrition!

Nielsen's 1998 survey indicates the six reasons why companies lose customers:

- 1 percent of customers die.
- 3 percent of customers move away.
- 5 percent are influenced by others.
- 9 percent are lured by competition because of price or some other issue.
- 14 percent are dissatisfied with the quality of the product or service.
- 68 percent feel rejected by an attitude of indifference on the part of an employee.

What this says about the experience the customer needs and wants is that you can do everything right...have the best product, the best price, the best location , the best selection, and lose your customers because of some erring employee.

Regina was much more painful than the dentist's drill

Regina was a bitter woman who worked for a large dental practice. Her function was office manager but her worth to the practice had been decreasing for many years. She had lost her husband, her daughter didn't pay much attention to her, and she was tired of working. In fact, she had taken a leave of absence (much to the delight of the senior members of the practice) but had returned because the office gave her a sense of purpose and importance and the dentists didn't have the heart to get rid of her.

Because Regina was the front line person, she had both the responsibility and the ability to create first impressions for new patients and good impressions for existing patients. What happened was that the rate of attrition for the practice was higher than average and, even through referral sources and aggressive promotions, the practice was not growing. In fact, the opposite was occurring. With 25 people on board, this dental corporation had a big problem...only no one knew the problem was Regina—including Regina!

A management consultant was brought in and several of the staff and dentists signed up for seminars by the experts in dental marketing, patient retention, and practice profitability. The management team brought Regina to many of the seminars. The office staff had become so accustomed to Regina's indifferent personality that they were blind to the problem. The dentists knew she wasn't as much of an asset as she once was, but they, too, were hazy about how caustic she could be. And, so the practice's business continued to decline...until a patient spoke out.

Andrea Collins liked the dentist she was seeing but was continually made to feel uncomfortable by Regina's tone. The straw that broke the camel's back was when Andrea questioned some of the forms for insurance reimbursement and Regina reacted with a contemptuous attitude. Andrea immediately asked to see the person in charge of the practice and was told by Regina that she was in charge. Andrea left in a hurry but decided to write to the dentist she was seeing in the practice. When Dr. Armand received Andrea's letter, he called a meeting of the senior staff with the exception of Regina. Once the door was opened to the issue of Regina, the floodgates were swelling with similar tales of woe about her behavior—not only with patients but with staff. The problem was evident, Regina was single-handedly ruining a $12 million dollar business...one patient at a time.

Needless to say, the necessary steps were taken and Regina was given a generous severance arrangement. Next came the task of finding the right person—having them thoroughly screened in order to assure that they would not repeat history.

When Rick Phillips talks about hiring nice people, he refers to an ad in the *New York Times* that said, "We don't teach our people to be nice...We simply hire nice people."

Auditioning the finest talent to join the team

Well, that's an interesting twist on an old theme...but then who sets out to hire mean-spirited people? I recently saw a large window sign in a gourmet supermarket that read, "We're auditioning the finest talent to join the team." The idea of an audition appealed to me as a first step in attracting people for a variety of jobs. The problem with hiring minimum wage workers or basic labor is that it's tough to inspire them to stay...and even tougher to train them to perform admirably.

Phillips's philosophy includes a demonstration that the customer is the boss. The idea is to motivate employees to get the customer to love the experience...and nothing motivates better than incentives like money, travel, or recreational products.

Recently, I suggested that a large group of automobile dealerships send the spouse of the salesperson a gift after each successful sale. In addition to the standard commission arrangement, a dozen roses was a standard to wives of salesmen...and a brand name cologne set to the husbands of the saleswomen in the organization. But it didn't end there. The next step was to establish goals that would be based upon customer reactions to that specific sales experience—whether the customer actually purchased the automobile or not. The idea was to let the sales staff know that their performance wouldn't be based solely on sales...but on the creation of an experience that delighted the customer.

Once the plan was in place, monthly reviews were established with each member of the sales force in order to assess their extreme customer service behavior. The customers were given a small premium for responding and a chance at a larger prize during a monthly drawing. Compliance was extremely high because the customer could vent their frustrations or praise efforts—while receiving a valuable incentive for themselves.

Treat employees as you would have them treat your customers

Employees are your customers, in a manner of speaking. By creating a powerful experience for your employees, you are creating an environment in which they will thrive. Extreme behavior toward employees means management must walk around, get to know each employee, and, if your organization has a large number of employees, establish times when the owner and a group of employees get together for a communal conversation...real talk, real issues, real problem solving, real fun.

If the employee understands and recognizes the critical connection between them and the customer, the company will win. That objective must be conveyed to every single member of the team from the maintenance staff to the upper management to the CEO. Motivating a labor pool of teenagers and people in their early twenties is not easy. But, if your business relies upon low-cost labor, you need to find creative ways of making these people work for you in a way that works for your customers. To begin with, look at the little details that turn teenagers on.

A friend of mine runs a business that employees six young people (18 to 22 years old). He can't afford to pay them a great deal of money, but he can afford to feed them and that's what he does. Each day, he takes lunch orders and pays the for the entire team. In fact, he discourages them from bringing lunch—because he always allows them to get what they want from a variety of local places. Not only do they love letting him pick up the tab, but he loves the fact that they now don't leave the premises during lunch—ensuring that they will adhere to their 40-minute lunch window. It's a great win-win solution.

In addition, bonuses are delivered monthly based upon performance and comments from customers. The bonuses are gift certificates to the Gap, Abercrombie + Fitch, Sports Authority, and so forth. They can bank their bonus points in order to reach a grand premium of a mountain bike, surfboard, and other gifts that are published in the company newsletter. The employees have one goal and one goal only. It doesn't relate to sales, profits, or company growth. Their only goal is to delight the customer and 40 plus percent of the customers fill out an "experience card," which asks three questions about their experience with the company.

EXPERIENCE CARD

1. Did you get exactly what you wanted? _____
2. Were you treated as a valued guest? _____
3. Would you come back and do business with us again? _____

Comments: ______________________________

____

____

If the team member recognizes that management will continue to ask about the experience, their behavior runs high. In addition, if a young person shows up for work and is lethargic, depressed, anxious, angry, or shows any signs of agitation, he or she is sent home for the day and docked pay. The first order of business each and every day for this entrepreneurial business is a prework interview. The owner spends a few minutes with each team member asking how they're feeling and revving them up. Like a huddle, they all get together before beginning the day's work and focus on the only goal they have for the entire day...making the customer smile!

- Ask yourself what techniques you're using to create extreme service behavior.
- What is it that truly motivates your customer to continue to do business?
- If you don't know, find out.
- What crazy ideas have you considered?
- Did you invite your team to come up with suggestions that will delight the customer?
- What have you done for the customer lately that they can't expect anywhere else?

Top/down management leads to bottom-line attitudes

Extreme customer service begins with behavior from the top down, as I have explained earlier. The first step in establishing an extreme posture is to define what the customer wants—but don't be fooled by this. Even when we ask this question, the customer doesn't always tell us what he or she wants. The fact is that many business owners today feel as if they already know what the customer wants...and they don't need to listen anymore. In addition, many employees view this attitude as apathy for the customer by their boss. The customer needs need to be anticipated—not reacted to. How many business owners today are actively prognosticating the trends in their own industry? Indeed, how many are actually paying attention to the trends in their own industry? If you don't, you may not have a future.

I do a great deal of work in the jewelry industry—both in manufacturing and retail. At many of the seminars I give, I ask a series of simple questions:

- If 80 percent of your customers are female in this industry, why are 80 percent of you attending this seminar male?
- How many in this audience read *Cosmopolitan*, *Vogue*, *W*, *Women's Wear Daily*, and so forth?
- How many of you read the trade publications for your own industry?
- What is it about your retail environment that is designed to excite the customer?
- What single issue sets you apart from your competition in the treatment of the customer?
- How often do you tell the customer how much you appreciate their business?

To begin with, not one of the people in the room has ever admitted to reading the consumer publications that their primary customer reads (and I've spoken to hundreds of groups). And, while approximately 50 percent read the trade magazines, most admitted that they look at the ads instead of the articles.

As far as the retail environment is concerned, only a handful in the past few years have done anything more innovative than reupholstering their chairs. What about coffee, cookies, espresso—even hairdressers offer their customers that much. They're selling high-ticket items with no window dressing, no value added environmental issues at play, or no system of telling the customer that he or she is your reason for existence.

As far as a single issue setting them apart from their competition, I've never had a creative response worthy of publishing in this book. When I ask how often they tell the customer how much they appreciate them...the answer is usually, "I always say 'thank you, have a nice day.'" They're not responsible for their nice day! They're responsible for offering them real, tangible, extreme service that customers will remember them by. What about lifetime free repairs, free watch batteries, repairing any defect, free insurance on the diamond for the first year of ownership, remembering their birthday, anniversary, gifts for their new baby—real issues that recognize the customer as their lifeline. "Have a nice day" is the easiest out businesses have in addressing what they think is a customer service issue.

I've told clients that each and every person in their organization has a responsibility to get a smile from a customer in a nonintrusive, nonaggressive way. Guess what it takes to get a customer to smile? A smile! Try it—this really works. If a customer enters your store, simply smile—don't even say a word. The mere fact that you have expressed warmth with a facial gesture will put a customer at ease and create a "conditioned response." This conditioned response is caused by engaging the customer and inviting a response. People respond in kind because a lack of response suggests indifference. Most people don't want to be indifferent to nice people.

Why would we take the customer for granted?

Indifference. It's a frightening word. Insensitivity is an equally frightening word. Look at industries that have suffered severe losses because of indifference. The banking industry is a fine example. So are the airline industry, supermarkets, soft drink companies, fast food restaurants, convenience stores, the corner bagel store, and so forth and so on. All of these businesses merely fill out orders from customers...instead of truly serving them. Because many of you are in entrepreneurial businesses, let's focus on a start-up success story: Dave's Bagels, in a suburb of Philadelphia. Dave started out highly motivated and enthusiastic. He wanted to please the customers in his quest to make it in his own small business. So, Dave attended a seminar I gave at a large bookstore and asked to chat for a few moments after my speech.

Dave was burned out. He loved the ideas but was having trouble understanding how he could grow his business and increase his wealth. He said, "if I stay at the same level of business, I'll never get what I want out of life." In order to feel motivated, the business owner has to see the light at the end of the tunnel.

So we got creative...and extreme in our thinking. We asked customers what they wanted and many said, "I love bagel sandwiches, but the ingredients always spill out onto my lap, especially when I'm in the car." The other comments consistently reflected the attitudes on the part of men, mostly, "when I want a sandwich, it's got to be big...I don't want some little bagel wrapped around my roast beef and cheese." Through such customer intervention and comments, Dave was able to invent the "no-hole" bagel and the "giant bagel."

Signs were posted in the windows and on the available walls which teased the customer, "What else can we do with a bagel that hasn't been done before...tell us and win a dozen bagels a week for a year!" The details to the offer suggested that if the store actually uses the idea or tests the idea, the customer gets a dozen bagels free for a full year. The customers loved it and it began a dialogue of jokes, real ideas, funny slogans, and a rapport that would never have been accomplished by simply selling bagels.

Admittedly, these surveys were grass roots, but they were consistent. We also recognized that the customer mostly ate the bagel sandwiches in the car or at work...not in the bagel store. So, we sat down and decided that we would remedy the problem, address the customer and create proprietary products that would meet and exceed their needs...thus the creation of the "Giant Bagel" and the "No Hole Bagel." What the concept did was to focus attention on the store and differentiate it...but the other issue was that we had fun with the adage, "you asked, we listened!"

First, we addressed the issue of product. Dave loved bagels and he was good at making good bagels. He also loved the notion of asking customers what they wanted and offering them any innovative idea that would distinguish him with existing customers and invite new customers to change "brands" and come to him. The product review began by looking at competitors and judging varieties. We found some creative bakers who were baking bagel flats (a flat, crunchy bagel), bagel twists (bagel pretzels), bagel kisses (shaped like Hershey kisses), and bagel bread (loaves of bread made with bagel dough). Since none of these products existed in Dave's market, we considered adding some of them to the product line.

Then we decided to ask customers what they loved about bagels. We ran ads in local papers which asked the customer to describe the perfect bagel, and for each response brought in to Dave's Bagel Store, Dave would give away six bagels absolutely free—no purchase necessary. The perfect bagel was a concept designed to get the customer to describe what they absolutely loved about the product, but it was also designed to get the customer to understand that Dave truly cared about the customers' opinions...more than his own.

The results literally rolled in (pardon the pun) and hundreds of people showed up in the first week of the advertisement. The suggestions were amazingly creative and targeted: 56 percent of the customer responses liked a bagel that was crunchy on the outside and soft on the inside, 30 percent liked bagels to be well done so that the inside wasn't mushy, and many other suggestions came in as well. In addition to the consistency of the bagel, many customers loved the idea of a larger bagel, a no-hole bagel, a bagel pizza, herb bagels, nutri-bagels, energy bagels, walnut bagels, peanut butter bagels, a bagel express delivery service...the list was wonderfully creative and diverse. The contest was ongoing and the responses were phenomenal. Dave gave away a lot of bagels...but at seven cents a piece, who cared? The assets far outweighed the liability. For several months, Dave tested a variety of suggestions, and about six new products were launched. He also was the only bagel baker we know of in the history of bagels to offer lightly-baked, regular, and well-baked bagels. Customers loved it! There was a bit of confusion at first until the staff got into the swing of things, but his customer base grew by 28 percent and bottom-line profits grew equally.

The other thing that happened was that Dave grew—personally and professionally. He had a higher profile as a brand in his market, new plans for a second store are underway, and he's having fun again. Every single day he enters his business he asks his employees for ideas...anything at all. He rewards them with hours off, days off, free bagels for their families—each and every time they get a customer to smile and fill out a "how are we doing" card.

Pricing was the next order of business. This one was easy. Every bagel store in the area was charging 50 cents for a regular bagel and 65 cents for a "specialty" bagel. Dave decided that his new pricing policy would be 45 cents for any bagel, with a baker's dozen every time. Dave's profit margin decreased slightly but his volume continues to climb.

Dave developed a policy of doing business with the customer. First, the policy included a frequent "biter" plan which offered free bagels after so many purchases, which was no big deal. The second policy was his freshness guarantee: If it's not fresh, it's free! Dave reminded customers that his bagels were discarded every six hours and his coffee pots were emptied every 20 minutes so that, if a customer even questioned the freshness of the product, it was offered free. In six months, he's only been taken advantage of twice—by the same person. The asset far outweighs the liability. Dialogue with the customer and ongoing goodwill (and fun) are what propels Dave forward. His plans for a second store include a bigger food and deli department and a bakery. The increased volume from his first store captured the attention of the local bank, which will be financing the new store. For Dave, revitalized customer service led to more profit and greater quality.

Chapter 6

Customer Service Starts With Common Sense

The illustration on page 94, "The Arc of Triumph," is an extreme customer service paradigm that is a simple behavioristic system that should be used by everyone who comes in contact with customers. If followed correctly, the Arc stands as a symbol of liberation and freedom from the mundane, mediocre, or modest treatment of customers.

The Arc of Triumph is not all inclusive, but rather is an outline of a system that is designed to make the customer feel triumphant and make you look heroic. Almost every industry could use simple, no-brainer issues to counter customer discontent. The Arc of Triumph is a system designed on the principle of common sensibilities.

Airlines are losing customers...when they should be landing them!

"Air rage" is the new term for disgruntled customers acting out in bizarre (and sometimes not-so-bizarre) ways. I clearly don't condone violent, abusive behavior by anyone, be they airline employees or passengers, but it truly is amazing that nice, ordinary people on both sides of this controversy can be pushed to rage by indifferent behavior.

The Arc of Triumph

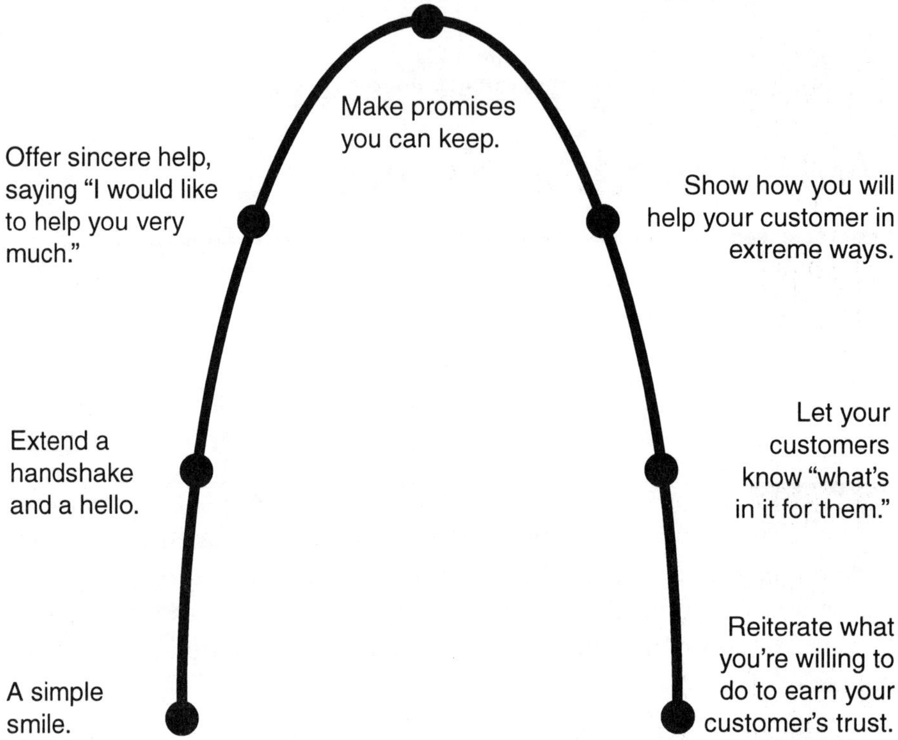

Make promises you can keep.

Offer sincere help, saying "I would like to help you very much."

Show how you will help your customer in extreme ways.

Extend a handshake and a hello.

Let your customers know "what's in it for them."

A simple smile.

Reiterate what you're willing to do to earn your customer's trust.

Recently, a young man and his family were attempting to board a plane for Orlando for a family vacation at Walt Disney World. The airline employee sent them to the back of the line because of a misunderstanding about the number of boarding passes. During the encounter, the couple's young child broke free and ran into the rampway heading for the plane. When the father started after his son, he was stopped by the employee, who presumably grabbed him. The father wrestled the employee out of his way in order to give chase to the young child. The man was charged with felony assault.

I've seen big abuses on the part of the airlines. I've encountered unpleasant ticket agents, unhelpful flight attendants, and arrogant employees at every level of the organization. It's incomprehensible that any company (indeed an industry) could care so little for their customers.

It was only a short time ago when "the friendly skies" were a prevalent theme in advertisements. All types of expressions of trust and friendliness were given by airlines to woo, wow, and invite us to their brand. What happened? Well, monopolistic ownership and thinking have been the death of many airlines over the past 20 years. An attitude has prevailed in the industry saying, "What else are people going to do—walk?" The attitude is fueled by the fact that in a very real way there's very little in the way of options when it comes to long distance travel.

The airlines are overbooked and the public is flying more frequently than ever. With a strong economy, travellers want to fly away to warm climates in winter, cool climates in summer, and on and on. The airlines have absolutely no interest in training employees in the art of customer service. It's almost evident that their training is in the art of offensive behavior or an attitude of "don't bother me, I'm busy."

Training is expensive...and the airlines have acknowledged that they are in the business of moving people in a physical way, not an emotional one. Amazingly, it's an industry that should excel in customer service because it, like the healthcare industry, needs to remind itself that the customer or patient is often anxious, nervous, and frightened. What does it take to be kind? What does it take to train people who are interacting with people as their primary job...a little understanding? The answer is that it takes a program and a conscience and the airlines have no room for either.

Are there people who abuse the airlines? Absolutely! They should be dealt with to the full extent of the law. But what happened to simple civility, caring, concern, and compassion? They exist to a very limited extent and they exist without a policy on the part of the airlines to delight the customer because they know that if they have the route and the schedule, they don't need to do anything else.

I'll teach airlines civility in 1 day—for free!

Here's my offer. I'll train the human resource people how to treat customers and build loyalty—for a full day for free! Are there any airlines out there willing to take me up on my offer? Call me, write me, e-mail me. I'll make the arrangements, waive my per diem, and invite you to my conference room for a full day of exercises and training on extreme customer service. Here's my number: 1-888-440-3367. Ask for me, it's toll free.

Engaging the customer is a matter of attachment

In her book, *Customer Loyalty*, Jill Griffin speaks of the issue of attachment as a prerequisite to loyalty. I often speak about "adhesion," which is a product or service identity that is "stuck" to the product in such a way that it draws immediate identification. Griffin is speaking about a similar notion, but she relates it to the attachment of a customer to a product or service. Her thesis has to do with the attachment a customer feels toward a product or service in terms of the degree of preference and differentiation. Attachment to a business by a customer occurs in the highest form when the customer has a strong preference for a product or service and differentiates it from competitive products.

An good example of attachment would be a New Jerseyan who drives 68 miles for a cleaning to the dentist he or she left behind in Brooklyn, New York. While this may be time-consuming, the attachment is so strong to the service that the patient/customer is willing to trade convenience and money for a strong preference.

If we become attached to a business, it often has to do with the kind of service we expect and receive consistently. If the dentist is caring, gentle, friendly, and kind, time and money issues are greatly desensitized by the distinct advantages of dealing with a nurturing individual, rather than experiencing the anxiety associated with starting a new relationship. If, on the other hand, a new relationship begins with these "attachment" issues high (kindness, caring, nurturing), then loyalty exists from the very beginning.

In business today, we want attachment with the customer and we want product and service identity to be pronounced. Interestingly, customer loyalty can remain high even when the product or service is not regarded as the best. This is where extreme customer service issues can perpetuate "attachment" even when the product is not perceived as being as strong as it could be.

Legal ease

Mike Travers is a feisty attorney. He works alone except for his paralegal, Cindy, and his administrative assistant, Judy. Mike is not the most pleasant person to deal with but he's smart enough to understand his shortcomings and he works hard on his attorney/client behavior. He's also smart enough to recognize that Cindy Caputo is his best asset when it comes to keeping clients "attached" to him. Cindy handles 90 percent of the client inquiries, phone calls, correspondence, communication, and hand-holding. She reassures clients who are apprehensive about litigation, she relates all the pertinent information in a calm, professional manner, and she shmoozes far better than Mike could ever possibly shmooze. Admittedly, Cindy is worth her weight in gold...and Mike is smart enough to pay her handsomely for keeping his clients loyal to the practice.

Cindy came to him one day and told him that she wanted to go to law school. Because Cindy is such an asset, Mike convinced her to attend law school under one condition—that he would pay for her schooling, give her the time necessary to attend classes, and tend to her studies (two afternoons off each week during exams)...but she promised that she would sign an employment contract upon completion of her bar exam that would guarantee that she would work as his associate for a period of three years. If she agreed to the terms of the contract, all her educational expenses would be taken care of by Mike and he would not seek any reimbursement. Mike is a smart lawyer and a smart businessman. He recognized that Cindy's value to him as a paralegal was quite high, but her value to him as a lawyer would be even higher. The issue of attachment was far more pronounced on the part of the clients who were made aware of the arrangement and the fact that Cindy was on her way to becoming a lawyer.

Why people buy

Jill Griffin's thesis points out some issues that summarize her theory on attachments; they're worth illustrating here. The points made communicate some of the differences between being proactive and reactive in behavior toward the customer.

- Every time a customer buys a product or service, they are advancing through a "buying cycle." Each step of the buying cycle is an opportunity to plant seeds of loyalty in an effort to create a cumulative customer service initiative.

- Depending upon the type of product or service involved, a customer may repeat the purchase a few times or many thousands of times in the course of the relationship. Each time a customer repurchases a product or service from a business, an opportunity exists to reinforce and strengthen the bond with the customer. Of course, there's also a possibility of weakening the bond with the customer if customer service issues are not consistent and exciting.
- A customer's level of attachment coupled with the level of repeat purchase defines the condition of loyalty. If the customer is consistently treated to a high level of service and repeats the purchase frequently, the bond is strengthened by the quality and frequency of extreme customer service. This customer is "attached" to the business. There's very little chance of losing the customer to another brand or business if their expectations are continually met—if not exceeded.
- There are four types of attachment: No attachment, latent attachment, inertial attachment, and premium attachment. **No attachment** means that the customer has not been given enough reasons to remain loyal to the product or service. **Latent attachment** means that there is a relatively high attitude toward the product, but with few repeat purchases. This is exemplified by a couple where the wife loves Nissan automobiles and has a high level of attachment to the brand and the dealership. Her husband doesn't like buying anything other than American brands and convinces her to change her loyalty and not repeat her purchase of the Nissan. **Inertial attachment** exists when there's a low level of attachment but a high repeat purchase pattern. This customer buys simply out of habit and convenience. An example would be the consumer who continually stops for gas at the corner station—not because of loyalty, great service, or even brand awareness—but simply because it's a pattern of convenient behavior. **Premium attachment** is the most potent of all four types, and exists when a high level of loyalty and repeat patronage coexist.

Griffin's contention is that premium attachment or loyalty can be achieved by a program called "Loyalty Management." In essence, loyalty management occurs when a business owner or manager assesses the potential loyalty of the customers based upon the behavior. For example, we know that we can manage loyalty by creating quality experiences which cause the customer to return to our business frequently based upon experience—not just convenience.

In my first book, *Start Up Marketing*, I spoke at length about the creation of quality experiences. The premise of extreme customer service is, at its very essence, about creating experiences that customers will remember as beyond pleasant or satisfactory...and beyond belief! There's a quote worth repeating from *Start Up Marketing* that is attributed to Kaoru Ishikawa from his work titled, *The Incredible Power of Cooperation*. Ishikawa states, "Why fight among yourselves when you can unify and win?" Unification is a principle of marketing that allows both the buyer and the seller to win. By allowing both parties to feel great about the transaction, loyalty is earned and a keen desire to repeat the relationship experience occurs. Discipline is a key ingredient to a win/win scenario for the buyer and seller. We must constantly remind ourselves that as sellers we have to fall in love with the customer, not the product or the sale. If our discipline includes true reverence for the customer and his or her wishes, desires, needs, and passions, then extraordinary loyalty will be built and riches can be earned.

Do you need an example? How about this principle applied to the Disney organization? Extreme customer service is a premise upon which the Disney organization was founded. Disney's four disciplines are listed in order of their priority of doing business:

1. Safety.
2. Courtesy.
3. Show/entertain.
4. Efficiency.

Disney owns all of these disciplines in the marketplace. You can test them by phone, mail, or in person. I did. Two years ago, I drove to Walt Disney World with my family. Upon arriving at the Polynesian Resort, I unloaded my minivan with the help of the staff and parked it. I noticed that the interior light on the van would not go out regardless of the switches, doors, and even a swift kick to the bumper. After a frustrating 15 minutes, one of the staff called the Disney Auto Repair Center and told them I would be arriving soon...even though they were closing in a few minutes. When I arrived, they treated me with extreme courtesy and solved my problem. Upon returning and joining my family to begin our vacation, each member of the staff who knew my problem (I think there were about six) asked me if everything was okay and apologized that I had a problem at the outset of the vacation.

Every time I appeared in their presence, they would make sure that everything was okay with the van. Were they paid extra to ask? I don't think so. However, it showed that they were trained in civility, cooperation, and the spirit of the Disney culture. Decisions are easy when values are clear. The marketing decisions made by an organization are quite simple once a philosophical attitude has been established and a discipline adopted.

If the airline employees could only fly as ordinary customers, perhaps they would gain a sense of service. If the doctor could only understand how anxious a patient can be made to feel when he or she is treated with indifference, perhaps behaviors would change and bedside manners would be better. If the store owner could jump across the counter and disguise him or herself as a customer—perhaps attitudes would then be appropriately adjusted.

Watch out—your customers may be out to help or hurt you!

Think about the impact a good experience can have on your business. Approximately one-third of your customers will relate a positive experience to friends, acquaintances, and/or family members. They are your "ambassadors." Interestingly negative news travels farther and faster. More than two-thirds of the people affected by a negative experience will happily relate that experience to anyone who will listen. The moral of the story: Do unto others as you would have them talk about you! To help you pinpoint how you treat customers, here are the four possibilities that exist today in the treatment of customers:

1. **Negativity.** You've just created an adversary and the word of mouth "trashing" can undermine everything else you may do right in your business.
2. **Indifference.** This is the most caustic attitude you can exhibit toward a customer. It communicates that you not only don't care, but you don't need their business.

3. **Positivity.** Being positive by creating a positive impression is a process that will win the customers' loyalty for life.
4. **Elation.** By saying or doing something so powerful that it elicits a smile and a gesture of warmth and nurturing, you've just succeeded in surpassing any features or benefits a product could offer—you've sold yourself to the customer!

Relationships create prosperity...not products. The attachment a customer has to a product is created by the total experience of purchasing the product, not just the consumption or use of the product.

Remember, most customers will abandon the relationship if they don't feel excited from time to time. The cost of mistreating a customer or simply satisfying the customer is great. The cost of winning customers back is even greater. A quality experience begins the first time a customer is made aware of a product or service. It is imparted in the tone of voice, the attitude, the point of view taken by the business owner, the copy, the graphics, the language and the style of communication—both through advertising and in person.

Let's review our extreme customer service checklist:

1. Do you continually review the experience you're offering the customer?
2. Do you empower the customer to make an informed purchase decision?
3. Do you offer a warranty or a guarantee?
4. Do you enter the buy/sell arena armed with the goal of creating a win/win situation?
5. Do your employees convey your philosophy of "do anything to make it right"?
6. Do you continually assess the competition in order to maintain a higher degree of service and product integrity?
7. Do each of your team members have the authority to make the customer happy?
8. Do all of your team members shake off the outside world before interacting with your customers?
9. Do you continually ask customers how you're doing and what really makes them happy?
10. Do you give customers at least three things they didn't ask for?

Sweet success

Jim Reynolds runs a wonderful store. It's called "The Chocolate Drop Peanut Shop." In it, you'll find a wide variety of the most indulgent edibles anywhere. You'll also find a wide variety of the most indulgent people anywhere. Why? Because indulgence is what makes Jim and his company great. The passion they feel about customer service is unequalled. They also feel passionate about the product. The poster on the wall communicates the philosophy of the company: "Life is short. Eat dessert first!"

When you walk into the shop, you feel as though Willie Wonka has taken you by the hand and has waltzed you into a world of fantasy. The colors, shapes, and sizes of candies, cookies, cakes, desserts, peanuts, exotic nuts, and fanciful chocolates are all designed to delight your senses. Jim and his merry bandits dress up like court jesters with bells on their hats and with a rainbow of colorful bandanas and scarves. Many members of the team wear hand puppets to hand the purchase over to the customer. Along the way, you'll get a great deal of help selecting your treats...and you'll get a great presentation of unique and unusual sweets.

In truth, Jim does what he loves and makes a great living. But he makes a great living because of his team—not because of his product. Every single item is available elsewhere in other gourmet emporiums, sweet shops, or dessert stores. However, you'd never know it because you wouldn't recognize the products anywhere else. Why? They're given personality and panache because of the surroundings and the service. Here's what I mean:

You order a simple quarter pound of chocolates. You're charged $3.67. The employee asks you a simple question: "Which three flavors of our candy sticks would you like?" You respond, "I'm not interested in buying anything else." But, the employee isn't selling you anything else, she's *giving* you three things that you haven't asked for...and she quickly tells you that. Would you believe that about 25 percent of those offered the candy sticks decline the offer? Mostly that occurs because they don't feel worthy of it.

In truth, Jim's customers will often decline the offer, but they would be heartbroken if Jim or his merry staff didn't make the offer. It's part of what they love about the store. The creativity on the part of the staff make the experience fun and memorable. By the way, they never, ever hand the customer the package over the counter. They always follow the Nordstrom service policy of walking around the counter and greeting the customer with a handshake and the package. They also often get to the front door first, in order to let the guest out. They never say, "have a nice day." Their thank you is accompanied by a little note that is included in the package as well as a verbal offering that imparts their pleasure in serving the customer. The employee simply says, "I've truly enjoyed seeing you and would love to serve you again as soon as your sweets run dry." The note card offers a whimsical thank you. It says:

> *"I have truly enjoyed helping you select some sweet offerings. Goodness knows the world could use all the sweetness it can get...and in our world, your presence is greatly acknowledged and appreciated. I would love to see you again. Thank you for the pleasure of serving you."*
>
> —Bob Jeffries.

Each employee signs their cards before they pop them into the customer's bag. It is a sweet, simple gesture of personal service that is consistent with the environment and the extreme customer service agenda. Give your customers three things they didn't ask for and tell them how important they are to you. Get rid of the "have a nice day."

Get SMART

The idea of a SMART customer service story is shown by the five issues presented here:

S Specify what you are willing to do to win over your customers and share this with your entire staff.

M Measure the results of extreme customer service with customer surveys and incentives to get customers to respond to your inquiries.

A Agree with your entire company on the critical nature of service in your organization. Have an agreement posted on the walls of the business that details the spirit of service and its importance to the future of everyone in the company.

R Realize your goals by measuring responses in terms of comments, dialogue with the customer, and repeat business.

T Time the program so that each issue that relates to your extreme customer service initiative has a deadline. If you commit to delivering a product to a customer by a certain timeframe, then treat that issue with the seriousness it deserves. It is an example of the kinds of promises customers expect you to keep if you're serious about keeping them as customers.

Components for creating loving customers

The following examples show how to draw customers closer to our cultures by creating a strategy that recognizes the customer as the reason a business exists:

- The quality experience can only work when every single individual in your organization succeeds in creating intimacy with the customer in some way, shape, or form that is noninvasive and nonthreatening.
- If you focus first on the needs of the customer in your thinking, not on the needs of the organization —you will gain the attachment I spoke of earlier. The customer recognizes when his or her needs are being placed at the top of your priority list. They will respond in kind.
- Remember that change is a necessary component of success. Anyone in your organization who refuses to change cannot be considered customer driven. What *can't* you change in order to succeed?
- Create committees but call them "teams." Gather information and suggestions from the collective membership in your organization and recognize good ideas with rewards.
- Post your "customer-owned company credo" on your walls. Every team member should be reminded constantly that your company is customer owned...without the customer, the company would cease to exist. Corny? Perhaps. But it works to reinforce the simple issues that keep team members prepared every time they interact with the public.
- Pay careful attention to customer suggestions or staff recommendations. Post the best ideas on the walls of the office and acknowledge the author of the idea.

- Constantly reward team members for outstanding performance. If a customer offers praise regarding any employee, respond immediately with a reward that will acknowledge the employee's contribution to the company. The most appropriate rewards include extra days off with pay, a weekend away—all the way up to a one year lease on a car—for repeatedly performing in an outstanding manner.
- Wrap important memos in ribbons and dispense them to each team member requesting a response. The response can be dropped in a "response box" or could simply be a check mark that indicates that the team member has acknowledged receipt of the important information.
- Continually explain and repeat why extreme customer service is so vital to the health and well being of everyone in the organization.
- Quality experiences are a trickle down effort. Each leader in your organization must be visibly involved in the day to day issues that make the extreme customer service program a mandate in your company.
- Post progress reports that show customer activity, amount of customers, customer appreciation issues, as well as sales and profit trends, and encourage celebration from all team members when a customer reacts with enthusiasm to your company.

These issues should be incorporated into your everyday business life. When you reinforce your concept of being a customer-driven company, you set the stage for "rethinking" your mission, whatever it is.

What is a customer, after all?

The word *customer* is distilled from the word *custom*. Taken in this context, this an interesting way to look at your business. If you treat those who buy from you in a customized way, you are addressing their needs specifically in every transaction. Therefore, a customer is *never* a commodity and, as such, cannot be treated the same as the last person who bought something from you. This is truly a revolution in thinking about the way you do business.

If you develop a custom approach to each customer, you're saying to them, "let me solve your problem." The idea that every customer can recreate the rules of business is exciting because it gives you and your staff the opportunity to have fun being creative in either solving a problem, selling a product, servicing, or romancing the customer.

When Sam Walton, founder of Walmart, wrote his autobiography, he stated, "Customer loyalty is where the real profits in this business lie, not in trying to drag strangers into your stores for a one-time purchase based on splashy sales or expensive advertising. Repeat customers are at the heart of Walmart's spectacular profit margins."

Sam was a pretty smart cookie. For one thing, he always went into secondary markets in the heartland of America. It's where traditional values and notions worked well. But, this man of basic principles was brilliant. What he was saying was that if you treat each customer as an individual, if you walk around, and greet your store employees on each visit, and if you engender a sense of community among your employees, the customers will feel acknowledged and special.

Customizing *is* customer service. When you acknowledge a customer as a person with specific wants and needs, you are utilizing the principle of custom-marketing—a distinct part of extreme customer service. When a customer service issue arises, a customized solution should be offered. Sometimes it requires us to ask the customer, "Please tell us what we can do to make this right." While we want to offer direct solutions to situations that may arise, we also sometimes need to be blatant in asking what the customer feels will remedy the situation.

"I've always depended upon the kindness of strangers"

Actually, we are all placed in situations where we depend upon the kindness of strangers. At airports, at doctor's offices, at hospital emergency rooms, at gas stations, at ferry boats, at train stations, at the hair and nail salon—even in restaurants. In truth, as consumers, we put ourselves into the hands of others each and every day. We do depend upon the kindness of strangers for our physical and emotional well being and safety. We struggle to be recognized, we clamor to be treated well, and we search for comfort and care in everything we do. Imagine if we had a business relationship where everyone in the organization (even strangers) treated us as a friend. Could you possibly imagine the feeling of belonging we would get. How about the business owner who could keep most of the prospects who are attracted to his or her business? What if the closing ratio for a jewelry store owner could go to 50 percent from the national average of 22 percent? Imagine the wealth of opportunities that would afford!

A little bit of kindness goes a long way

When AT&T decided to be kind, they did so during the holiday season. The TV campaign showed a frightened teenager alone and bewildered on a dark city street. The voiceover said, "if you're a long way from home and you need to call your family...we can help. Pick up any phone and dial this number, we'll do the rest to get you in touch with your loved ones...and the call is on us." The kindness of this super-huge conglomerate played America's heart strings like a harp. It was brilliant marketing and it suggested that AT&T cares deeply about people during the holidays. My only concern is why isn't this offer reiterated year after year? Regardless, it was a noble effort at creating kindness.

Aamco Transmissions ran a campaign which offered child safety seats at cost...another attempt at appearing kind. And, indeed it was a kind offer. The idea that a company will do something for free—at little or no cost to the customer—is a wonderful example of what extreme customer service can do for the image and the "attachment" factor a business can enjoy.

Most people have a joker up their sleeve

For the most part, business owners are afraid to be taken advantage of. However, playing the fool can be a wonderful thing, if it is done correctly. Because employees are responsible for interacting with customers, managers should learn a lesson from some fine examples of tomfoolery in business. The idea that creative exercises can be perceived as foolish is perfectly okay. Many companies actually do silly, foolish things, such as encouraging an occasional food fight in the corporate cafeteria, a basketball game in the parking lot, or a management vs. worker paintball tournament. The foolhardy and fun facets of a business translate into spirit that goes way beyond the traditions of corporate incentives.

John Bennet owns a small printing company called Renaissance Printing that employs approximately 25 people. The company is right outside a large metropolitan area. Each day during lunch, some employees play volleyball in the back of the building. Picnic tables line the small grassy area next to the volleyball court. Those who don't choose to play volleyball, have a choice during their 70-minute lunch. They can shoot hoops in the parking lot, shoot billiards in the "lunch room," or play video games in the foyer of the printing shop building.

John plays basketball most of the time during lunch. Then, when the catering truck arrives, those who have not brought their lunch may head out to a local restaurant for a bite, or take advantage of John's generosity and get anything they want from the truck. Usually most people allow John to buy lunch and they eat together at the picnic tables.

John has a deal with the lunch truck operator. He is billed monthly for the purchases and his employees are incredibly grateful. Attrition at John's printing company is virtually nonexistent. There's only one catch to all of the extras John does for his team. They must live the law of Renaissance Printing: "Kindness to customers comes first, quality printing comes second. If a customer questions the quality, they are offered every solution possible—including preprinting—or their money back! If we miss a deadline, the printing job is free and we act delighted to deliver the free job!"

John's business has grown by $2 million in volume over the past year through this extreme policy of customer service. He knows the birthday of every customer who orders printing. For example, Evelyn, who is responsible for reordering hospital forms for the local healthcare facility, gets a dozen roses on her birthday, her anniversary, Valentine's Day and Mother's Day. Evelyn never forgets to call John and thank him for his kindness...and with orders.

Child's play at Wal-Mart

A commercial that Wal-Mart ran in test markets is an incredible example of extreme customer service. It begins with a young mother entering a Wal-Mart store. She is holding hands with two young kids—one on each arm. As she walks past the tall and dense racks of clothing, one of the kids breaks away from her grip and disappears within seconds. She is understandably panicked. Immediately the loud speaker blares out an authoritative male voice: "No one will be permitted either in or out of the store until Tommy Sanders is found." The next shot we see is a reunion between mother and child, with the smiling employee towing the child to Mom.

The concept of selling service instead of item and price is a brilliant way of illustrating to the world that Wal-Mart cares about what its customers care about most. Wal-Mart already communicates and owns the low price image...and the enormous variety image...and the computerized checkout technology image...even the friendly image. Now, it's going after the "we're going to take extra special care of you" image.

When a local realtor provides a certified babysitter to couples looking for new homes during evenings—that's extreme customer service. She pays for the service because it's her investment in the sales opportunity. It has developed her reputation for "extreme" personal service so that she's sought out three times more often than any other agent in the organization.

Here is another example. When my pair of Revo sunglasses became scratched to the point of visual distraction, I took them to a retailer who, in turn, gave me the address for the Revo company. I contacted them by phone and they suggested that I send them back. Upon receipt, I got a phone call from a customer service representative who explained that they no longer carried the lenses that would replace those particular frames. She said that they would be delighted to send me a new pair that was close to the old one for a nominal shipping charge. I told them I would send them a check. The next day, before I could even write the check, a FedEx package arrived. It contained my new glasses, a beautiful Revo hat, and a note thanking me for being their customer. They didn't even wait for the fee...and they won me over forever.

Imagine buying a Lexus and after two years needing tires? Hey—it happens. My dear friend Elaine loved her Lexus and brought it in for service and new tires (they were wearing thin on the outside). When she returned home later that day, her car was in the driveway with new tires and a note that simply stated, "We're sorry for the trouble...the tires are on us." Whether this was the individual dealer's decision or a corporate policy didn't matter to Elaine. She was hooked and she's on her second Lexus, soon to be on her third.

The most effective tool we have to keep our customers and gain new ones is the reputation we have for decency, integrity, honesty, compassion, and love! When companies truly exhibit these attributes, they win.

Chapter 7

Service Shmervice...All I Care About Is Price!

Is price important? Of course it is! Is quality important? You bet! How about location? Environment? The truth is, everything is important when you're competing in a cluttered marketplace. Most business owners will tell you that all the customer cares about is price. After all, they say, we're selling a commodity...aren't we?

The truth is that if we remember back a few chapters, you'll notice that "commodity" is a word we don't want to use in business today. Think about chickens *before* Frank Perdue. Did anybody brand chickens? Was there any consumer awareness regarding a difference between one chicken and another? Well, Frank came along and educated us about the differences between chicken, and he did so by telling us that he was watching out for us. Frank Perdue became our "chicken mentor," our friend, and our chicken-checker. He sold us on extreme service regarding a product that no one identified as having proprietary features. Did he talk about price? Never! He spoke about plumper chickens or more meat per pound...but the message alone didn't sell the lower cost of a Perdue Oven Stuffer.

Statistically, price as a selling issue is lessened as service is heightened. So, in simplistic terms, the better reputation you have for service, the less the buying public cares about price. Take Nordstrom, for example. Nordstrom is an anomaly in retail. Why? Because they turned to customer service as a primary selling proposition and succeeded.

What's the average sale at Tiffany's?

Take a guess at what the average retail sale price is at Tiffany's. Would you believe under $300? Isn't that absolutely amazing? The average sale at Tiffany's isn't $10,000 or $50,000—it's $289! Why? Because of people I call "aspirers!" Aspirers are consumers who are drawn to upscale service and products, but don't have the money to partake of them. But because they aspire toward better products and service, they will look for affordable items in exclusive environments. It's wonderful. I can remember shopping at Tiffany's some years ago. I looked at a bracelet that I thought was $1,700. For a moment, I thought about extending myself beyond my gift-giving budget for this wonderful bracelet. When I asked the salesman if they would take a personal check, he indicated that with proper identification that would be fine. Just as I reached for my checkbook, he queried me, "Sir, you are aware that it's $17,000, right?" "Of course," I replied. Not wanting to be embarrassed, I simply said that I would need to think about it before I made a final decision. He nodded with that slightly sheepish grin.

The moral of the story is that Tiffany's understands that its customer aspires to be its customer! The point of the story is that Tiffany's thrives on lower price-point goods because people want to purchase the brand. The price of a Tiffany's silver bracelet is high compared to a non-Tiffany's bracelet. Tiffany's makes much more on their silver bracelet than does the store down the street. But the panache, the service, the environment, and the reputation are what we're buying. Can service outsell price? Of course! But the message and the experience must be consistently excellent.

Tiffany's service includes the way in which you're treated—whether it's a $49 Tiffany's pen or a $49,000 Tiffany's necklace. All consumers expect the same treatment at Tiffany's and, to a degree, they probably get it. But the expectation of service stems from the Tiffany's history of excellence and sophistication. Who cares if you're spending more, you're enjoying it a whole lot more as well.

McDonald's versus T.G.I. Friday's

McDonald's has done a great job of distracting us from price. Aside from their "Extra Value Meals," price is rarely even mentioned on commercials! Sure, their reputation was built on economics many years ago.

But today, a family of four can easily eat at any leisure restaurant—Bennigan's, T.G.I. Friday's, Chili's, or Cracker Barrel—for about the same price as McDonald's. (Let's not leave out Wendy's and Burger King.) The fast food restaurants have led us to believe so strongly in their low prices that most of the consuming public cannot tell you what a Big Mac or a Wendy's double cheeseburger costs. The cost was never an issue until very recently when Extra Value Meals came into play. And, they only evolved when the fast food companies began to see softer sales. One way to motivate families back was to illustrate just how cheap it is to eat certain meals at their restaurants. Even at that, the cost is comparable to many sit-down, more traditional restaurants. Price sensitivity was never an issue for McDonald's. We were educated by their advertising to focus on an economical image, coupled with a consistent record in food service.

How do you turn a low-priced commodity into a brand?

A large regional corrugated cardboard manufacturer was in the process of trying to differentiate itself to achieve greater market share. The only selling proposition they had was price and the entire sales force was stymied by the frustration of this approach to getting orders. The first question asked at our first meetings was also the hardest: "How can you possibly market a brown box?" The purchasing agents who need boxes base their decision on price, right? Well...almost right. In truth, as we delved further into the culture of this industry, we discovered that price was essential but relationships were the primary reason purchasing agents remained loyal to one supplier over another. The ideal situation was to have a reasonably competitive price with a host of other value-added service components.

In truth, price was important. For that reason, all the other issues had to be fairly tangible in terms of a "reason to buy." So, the first suggestion I made was to look at branding a box differently by virtue of a value-added component which could soften the price sensitivity and produce better margins. Also, by branding a box, the manufacturer becomes an industry innovator instead of a mere commodity supplier. We did just that.

The first brand concept was to introduce "Corrutane," a coined word that combined "corrugated" and "container" into a brandable identity. Corrutane had to be different than a standard box in order to justify its existence. We went to work with the technical people to engender certain attributes into the Corrutane product in order to make it truly brandable.

First, Corrutane was tougher than a regular box because of a coating. Secondly, it was available in a variety of colors, which was uncommon to the industry. Thirdly, Corrutane carried a "structural integrity" guarantee. The product was invented to provide a focus on the company and to allow them to create an image that would differentiate them from the universe of boxmakers.

The price issue was deflated by the introduction of a value-added product...coupled with a value-added program. The service program that was also rolled out was compelling. If the product was not delivered on time, a large discount was applied for each day the shipment was late. Further, if you needed a customer service representative 24-hours-a-day, one would be available through a special service number. You would also be assigned a quality control clerk who would track the production of your order to ensure specifications, color, die cuts, and all other technical aspects of your job.

This overall effort proved that service in the form of both product branding and guarantees could reduce price sensitivity. It also proved that even a brown box wasn't subject to the cynicism that often accompanies the purchase of commodity goods.

Risk reversal defuses the perception of high prices

We talked about businesses assuming the risk in an effort to win the sale and overcome price sensitivity. During a recent appearance on CNN, I was asked what it would take for the NBA to overcome the bad feelings created by last year's strike. My answer included many different issues. First, a public apology to the fans and ticketholders. Second, free shirts, balls, sweatbands, and socks to all ticketholders. Third, free season replacement tickets...and to all the fans out there, a chance to win super giveaways for tuning back in.

Do sports enthusiasts care about the price of the tickets? No way! Do they care about the price of the hot dog at the stadium? Not really.

What they do care about is being taken for granted What this example illustrates is that enthusiastic customers will pay the price to get what they want. And, in the case of basketball...what they want is an exciting event! People care about price when the only selling proposition is a commodity one. Why buy a car from one dealer over another? Price, right? After all, the car is exactly the same. So, the way in which distributors of like products compete is by creating an extreme selling proposition that has nothing to do with the product...only the system of selling and servicing.

Robert Hayes, a professor at Harvard Business School, writes, "Fifteen years ago, companies competed on price. Today it's quality. Tomorrow it's design. Professor Hayes believes in the concept of passionate performance. His 1980 *Harvard Business Review* article, "Managing Our Way to Economic Decline" described the issue of the tedious analysis of business as a detriment to the passionate attachment people have to products and services. His thesis is that the quality of the service, product, or experience is much more revolutionary today—and is far more important to the consumer than price. By researching consumer habits, he has come to the conclusion that the next major trend in business is design...and not price!

Warren Blanding, editor and publisher of *Customer Service Newsletter*, states that, "...quality and customer service are a positive force for increasing sales, and for reducing the cost of sales." If customer service can reduce the cost of sales, why would companies think of it as an expense? Especially if we can prove that price sensitivity decreases when quality and service increase.

Fred Wieserma, author of *Customer Intimacy,* believes that a customer buys a product in order to achieve an entire set of satisfying experiences. Therefore, the supplier's goal has to be geared toward the experience the customer receives *before* price becomes an issue. This concept relates to an example of this that happened to me recently.

I entered a restaurant in a hurry to get out of the rain along with one of my associates. Nether one of us paid attention to the menu. All we wanted was a relatively modest meal in a casual environment. This restaurant appeared to fit the bill.

We were seated by a very gracious hostess who immediately brought over water, a dish of limes and lemons, and a tray of olives, vegetables, and dip. She asked us if we would like a drink, which we declined. The level of service seemed to outweigh the environment and we were pleasantly surprised.

We thanked her...only to see her return with a small tray of crackers and a horseradish cheese in addition to the crudites already on the table. We were enthusiastic about our accidental choice of restaurant.

When the menus arrived, we noticed that the prices were higher than we had anticipated spending for a quick lunch. However, the prices didn't bother us because of the extra special service we had received so far. We ordered sandwiches and salad. When the food was delivered, we were overwhelmed by the size and quality of it. Not only did the prices seem insignificant, they seemed too low, compared to the meal we were enjoying.

The service was extreme, with the waitstaff anticipating our every need. Water glasses were never permitted to get completely empty, new slices of limes and lemons always appeared, along with the invitation to enjoy a complimentary glass of the house dessert wine after lunch. If you asked me 20 minutes after this experience to tell you what the cost of the meal was, I couldn't tell you. I can only tell you that it was not enough.

In *Customer Intimacy*, Wieserma explains that it's the seller's goal to improve the entire spectrum of the experience...to make acquiring products and services more pleasant, to ensure that they're properly understood and used and to facilitate quick and effective remedies to any problems which may occur. After all, customers don't care about your problems—they only care about getting their own needs taken care of.

The 9-point solution

For years, clients have asked me to "Nordstrom" them or "Tiffany's" them. What they were saying was that they desperately wanted to be known for something special—something so special that people didn't haggle over price, kick tires and move on, or walk away because they were looking for their product cheaper. My nine-point solution is a list of issues that capture the customer's loyalty, without using price. The nine-point solution is designed to help businesses establish a creative services groundwork that creates an aura of excellence. Read the nine points below and see how each of them can help set your company apart from your competition:

1. Creating extreme excitement.
2. Breaking down the buy/sell barrier.
3. Creating true interactive dialogue.
4. Touching the customer both literally and figuratively.
5. Selling service before the product.
6. Including the customer in the buying decision.
7. Giving the customer what he or she wants, needs, and desires.
8. Creating intimacy through partnering up with the customer.
9. Communicate as a real person, not just a seller.

1. **Creating extreme excitement:** When we create real excitement, what we're doing is selling the experience beyond the product or service. It requires creative communication that focuses on the ultimate benefit of the product in order to make the product more exciting to the buyer. Obviously this needs to be created when selling a car...but even fire alarm systems can become exciting if you use anecdotes and examples of the product saving lives or property. Excitement is not always positive, but it moves people to action.

2. **Breaking down the buy/sell barrier:** Regardless of what we're selling, what we really want to sell is the *concept*, not our specific product or service. By selling the concept, we become teachers instead of salespeople, and people listen to teachers with greater interest than they listen to salespeople. For example, when I deliver a presentation, I never sell my company first. I always sell the enormous benefits of marketing. While doing so, I educate the potential client and also suggest that they consider a variety of options before deciding upon one firm. This is done with honesty and integrity...and it breaks down the buyer/seller agenda by moving the motivation to the side for a moment. I have often listened to a business owner discuss his or her needs and told them that before I could work with them, I would need to assess the feasibility of their success in their market. After

all, I don't want to be blamed for failure if their goals are unrealistic or their budget is inadequate.

3. **Creating true interactive dialogue:** The creation of real dialogue that involves the customer is significant. Real dialogue almost never has a sales tune associated with it. Instead, it follows the same form as informal conversation. We need to get to know the personalities associated with the transaction in order to exhibit an extreme customer service posture. If the customer is unwilling to speak with you, then your success in closing the sale will be difficult. By engaging the customer in a real conversation about the use of the product and why they even want the product, you are removing yourself from the realm of seller and taking on the role of fellow human being. Often, talking a customer out of a sale creates a loyalty that will increase their worth to you tenfold over the long term.
4. **Touch the customer both literally and figuratively:** I don't ever believe in touching anyone inappropriately or without provocation. When I have gently touched the arm or hand of a client to emphasize a point or to create an exclamation, I do so with great care. Obviously there are people who, for one reason or another, are uncomfortable with physical contact, and they make it abundantly clear. Human contact clearly illustrates intimacy and suggests that there is an emotional aspect to the relationship. Touching a customer emotionally is another part of this equation. We touch the customer by using body language, eye contact, and by our expressions. What we want is to allow the customer to understand that there is a sincerity to go beyond satisfying them...to truly give them value in the exchange of a product or service.

   My friend Ron is a wonderful insurance salesman. He spends most of his time in meeting with prospects asking them about their needs—financially and emotionally. He touches them with his interest in their lives and their sense of security. When he gets to the product that will ultimately protect them (the policy) he insists that they both understand and agree on the terms, the objectives, and the value of the policy.

Touching the customer places an immediate value on the relationship that supersedes other issues such as price, but it can only be effective when it's truly done with passion on the part of the seller. Ron loves people. If he didn't sell insurance, he would be in social work...his first love. People believe he cares because nobody's that great of an actor.

5. **Selling service before the product:** When you sell extreme service first, the product sells far more easily. If you are selling a car, you should discuss the free loaner, the pickup and delivery of the automobile for service, the repair program, the guarantees, the extra dealer incentives, the add-ons, and so forth...before the features of the automobile are even mentioned. Often, the customer doesn't even know why he or she wants a specific product. The customer is shopping for information he or she can use to make comparisons between brands or between dealers. If the initial conversation communicates extreme customer service, getting the sale is the next logical step.
6. **Including the customer in the buying decision:** When you include customers in the buying decision, you do so by asking them what they want, need, and desire. Remember, your job is to exceed their expectations, delight and wow them in the transaction, create loyalty, and have them desire to do business with you as often as possible. Ask them what they want from you. Most customers will tell you what they want. Then, you can use the information to exceed their expectations. The customer's needs, however, are something different. By figuring out what they need, you can open the door to a variety of options. What a customer may need is a dining room set to replace the card table which is there now. What he or she wants is a dining room table—but that's not necessarily what they need. So, if price, availability, size, or function are issues, then moving them to another possible "want" is possible. You don't lose the sale by not being able to give them exactly what they want.
7. **Giving the customer what he or she wants, needs, and desires:** Remember, desire is often stronger than reason for a sale. So, what customers *desire* is different from what they *want*

or *need* because it's totally driven by emotion rather than reason. You want the customer to get what they desire within reason...and it's your job to create a sales experience that delivers on all these three levels. If the customer wants the exact dining room table and price is no longer an obstacle, they may desire to have it delivered in time for their upcoming dinner party. They may also want it customized. They may want it stained another color, or maybe the chairs with a different color of fabric. You get the point. Clearly extreme service dictates that we give them what they desire. If we can't, then we need to get creative immediately. If you miss the delivery deadline, be on time with delivering the customer's first meal to be eaten on the new set which arrived a few days late!

8. **Creating intimacy through partnering up with a customer:** Becoming a partner with your customer is no more than listening, responding, acknowledging, and respecting him or her. The partnership begins when you promise to deliver. The customer understands that your business needs to make money, but he or she doesn't necessarily sympathize with businesses. So, it's important to break down such barriers immediately and to relate to customers as peers.

   Tom Porter owns a brokerage firm. He sells stocks and bonds, manages portfolios, and creates retirement plans. He approaches every investment as if it is his own. When he counsels clients, he does so as if they were investing their money as well as his. In fact, he often matches the investment recommendations he makes for clients for himself. So, on many occasions, he will buy stocks for clients alongside his own order for the same stocks. Clients truly believe (and rightfully so) that they are partnering with him.

9. **Communicate as a real person, not just a seller.** If you've ever wondered what makes Howard Stern so successful, it's really simple. He has never acted or sounded like a disc jockey in his entire career—He's only sounded like Howard. Love him or hate him, his success stems from the fact that he communicates as a real person, never as someone selling a message.

   When Richie Krinsky looks to close a sale at his very high-end jewelry gallery, he does so by speaking as one person to another.

He speaks about the guarantees, the integrity of the piece, the comparable value, the no fine-print return policy, and the beauty of the product itself. After all, he's a salesperson. But, in communicating these services and the product, he does so as a real person. He also suggests that the customer may want to think about the purchase or even take the jewelry home for a day or so in order to "live with it," or share it with a spouse. Being "real" to Richie also means pointing out the fact that the purchase is a big decision. The customer needs to know that if they ever have "buyer's remorse," there's a three-year money back guarantee. Furthermore, after the three years, they can receive store credit for the exact amount they paid (and if it's precious metal, they receive the upside if the value has increased...with no downside if precious metals have decreased). Not bad for a kid who started out selling gold chains at flea markets. His business now does almost $2 million worth of business per year.

People want value, but value doesn't only relate to price. Value is the quality of the experience one receives in a transaction. That quality can be far more driven by service issues than price...especially when comparable prices are competitive, not outrageous!

Chapter 8

Who Are These Customers...and Why Do They Say Such Awful Things?

Recently in *Business World,* an article asked some major questions on where businesses are in the field of customer service. The article referred to customer service in the public service areas as an oxymoron. After all, when was the last time you got service from the meter reader, the mailperson, the toll collector, or the bus driver? Nobody's wowed you in the public sector in a long time, I would dare say. Amazingly, the article also illustrated that while public service is not renowned for customer service, the private sector is doing a fairly inconsistent job with the same issue.

Argee Guevarra related his story about a trip to a Honda service center which he dreaded. He was exasperated by the price of repairs and parts but the service was fast, efficient, and hassle-free. In reminiscing about the experience, he admits that the cost vanished when the car was fixed quickly.

However, having left the Honda dealership, Argee was hungry. So, he stopped at Herb's Pizza for lunch. After waiting for more than an hour, Argee related to the waitress that his pizza was ordered over an hour ago, to which she replied, "It's only been 34 minutes, mister."

Recently when I visited a local library, the librarian related how quiet it's been. She guessed that many of the library patrons (not customers) were lured away by the big superstores. She was so surprised that people would prefer to spend money than to borrow books for free. I casually suggested that perhaps the library could generate more customers and more revenues by selling coffee and light snacks, much like the way Barnes & Noble does. Also, I suggested replacing the hard wooden chairs with comfortable sofas and loveseats. She laughed out loud. "No, I'm serious, " I said. She said, "You can't be serious." I asked her why not and she rolled her eyes in disbelief.

It's truly amazing to me that the thought of giving people simply what they've illustrated they want is foreign to some companies. The library system is a "company" entitled to produce revenues, expand services, and offer amplified products. Yet, the silly thought of modeling itself after a highly successful "retail library" such as Barnes & Noble is thought to be absurd.

Can customers truly love you?

Precision Marketing recently published an article which addressed the issue of "customer love." The article questioned the relative value of a customer who chooses to spend money regularly at your store or the customer who purchases at your store because there are no viable alternatives. The success of a program that cultivates the customer relationship is dependent upon the differentiation of these two issues. The concept of creating "loyalty schemes" has risen to an art form lately. Loyalty schemes are programs designed to get customers to fall in love, quite literally, with a business.

Recently, Pepsi ran a campaign where customers could send in 10 bottlecaps from Mountain Dew bottles along with $20 to receive a free pager. Doing this, Pepsi had direct access to some of their end users and continued to page marketing and advertising messages on a regular basis to these consumers. The relationship between the manufacturer and the customer is now enhanced and the purchasing behavior is used to gain loyalty.

Great Britain's Cranfield School of Management has recently created a model which they believe will help them understand how many of a firm's existing customers can genuinely be persuaded to change their purchasing behavior by means of customer service incentives, guarantees, and other issues. They created their "Diamond of Loyalty" classification matrix which divides customers into different categories and describes their purchasing behavior. Customers, according to this model, could be:

- **Switchers:** These are good customers with repeat purchase patterns who are not loyal to a brand and will generally be influenced by price.
- **Habituals:** Customers who will stick to a particular brand which they purchase out of habit and give very little thought to their decision.
- **Variety Seekers:** These customers love to purchase the product but will experiment with other brands just for a change.
- **Loyal Customers:** These customers will stick with a particular brand and have a high level of commitment to it.

The composition of categories will vary across product categories and industries. For example, in the breakfast cereal market, the number of variety seekers is very high, while in the newspaper industry, the number of loyal customers is high.

If you can apply your customers to this matrix, it helps you to understand how we can employ different tactics to secure a more loving, committed relationship with our customers and use extreme customer service issues to win over their hearts and minds.

Successful loyalty schemes have a common thread. They provide the customers with what they want, not what the manufacturer would like them to have. The classic example is Coca-Cola's enormous marketing error in creating a new Coke, then retreating to Classic Coke.

A.C. Nielsen, the reporting agency, recently completed an in-depth market research project on retail loyalty programs. They surveyed nearly 33,000 households and found:

- The majority of those joining a loyalty program do so for additional savings.
- Most present their "loyalty cards" on every shopping occasion.
- In most cases, frequent shoppers spend more per year than nonmembers.
- There appears to be a correlation between higher income levels, frequent shopper participation, and customer loyalty.

In Australia, a loyalty program has been introduced to encourage citizens to buy domestic products and services. The program is called "Advantage Australia," and includes some 30 or so companies from varying industries. Consumers who buy Australian products receive stamps in a passbook (remember Green Stamps?). A completed book entitles the customer to rewards such as sporting tickets, movie tickets, travel, and meal incentives. The idea is to get back to the times when gas station attendants wiped your windshield regularly, S&H Green Stamps were given out everywhere, banks gave appliances to thank you for depositing your money, and premiums were rampant in every industry.

In Germany, Texas-based Alamo Rental Car introduced their "True Blue" loyalty program that came undone when they discovered, much to their surprise, that it was illegal. Surprisingly, in Germany, you can give customers a gift—but only after they've purchased a product more than once. After altering the reward levels on its program, Alamo is back on track with its incentive plan to give customers a "thank you" gift for choosing them.

Stories from *Customer Service Review*

Here are some great statistics and information that I culled from *Customer Service Review*:

- Because customer-specific marketing was initiated in 1993, the average order size has increased by 25 percent and the customer attrition rate has dropped by 33 percent. This means that when a store communicates with customized mailings that address the specific customer ...based on the customer data, the response is enormous.
- When companies ask "What's wrong," customers come back. Companies who use their sales team to persuade customers to come forward with any grievances, complaints, or thoughts about the experience they had doing business with the company, they keep customers longer and increase the loyalty among them.
- Relationship services help keep customers! Many British companies, for example, have begun aggressive customer service programs that communicate with their customers by either

newsletters, letters, postcards, or other such mailings. This trend is catching on with travel industries, supermarkets, catering companies, and other industries. They publish "minimagazines" and mail them to customers on their database. The research indicates that there are now 20 British firms producing over 246 magazines for a worldwide readership of over 11 billion. Research has indicated that many people do not consider such mailings junk mail and that these promotional magazines create a level of customer connection that is more intimate and powerful than mass media advertising alone (such as TV or radio).

- Nestle launched the "Casa Buitoni Club," a quarterly magazine, and has found that the response is overwhelming. Letters they receive indicate that the customers appreciate and enjoy the contact that the company has made with them. The publication aims at giving more than information about pasta products; it also provides items of interest about Italian cooking, culture, music...and subtly encourages people to buy more pasta by increasing their knowledge. The editorial format is thoroughly readable (unlike most newsletters) and includes colorful, informative stories about Italian food. The club's database consists of about 200,000 people with individual profiles providing demographic details, shopping habits, and food likes and dislikes.

Getting lost in a voice mail nightmare

Technology is creating a dilemma for companies who believe that it will reduce costs and increase efficiency. Today, many companies have opted for voice-mail systems where it is virtually impossible to reach a live human being. Some time ago, I cancelled all of my company's insurance, including my personal lines. What is the reason? I spent two hours on any given day attempting to reach anyone live at the insurance agency. I drove the 45 minute ride to their offices in order to slam my fist on the table and demand my premium refund. There was no other way to accomplish the task other than doing it in person.

If your company uses a voice mail system, it's imperative that there's a quick link to an operator and that the tape offers that option up front.

If you don't, you run the risk of losing customers before you gain them. You should also ensure that the messages are inviting, friendly, and interactive—with immediate options to reach a customer service specialist.

Smaller companies without voice mail are far ahead of the customer service game. These companies can also gain a huge competitive advantage over others by advertising the lack of voice mail as part of their culture. The Internet and other new media need to evolve quickly toward a system of customer service that does not keep customers at a technological disadvantage when doing business. Customer service is an old-fashioned notion with no high-tech counterpart yet.

If you've ever had a problem with an ATM and it has eaten your card, you know the frustration of attempting to get a "real" person to respond. In some cases, it's impossible...especially if you're dealing with the computer after normal banking hours. I realize that technology is changing the business landscape faster than anyone can imagine, but extreme customer service issues are still human issues and, for entrepreneurial businesses, there's nothing as critical as human spirit, contact, and personality.

Close to losing your "satisfied customers"?

Barry Maners of Matrix Marketing in Indianapolis suggests that, just because your current customers seem happy with you, don't get too comfortable. For one thing, your competitive edge with existing customers may, in fact, be misleading. Matrix's research focused on existing customers and pointed out that customers are only claiming satisfaction with what they are currently receiving—not what they could receive. This explains why customers who claim they are satisfied with a specific enterprise's product then turn around and defect to the competition.

What is needed, according to Maners, is "customer value management." This research approach enables the company to analyze its own strengths and weaknesses by assessing the enterprise's competition. Customer value management measures the key success factors which form the basis on which the customer will evaluate the company's product in relation to that of its competitors. These factors include product quality, costs, service acquisition, usage, and image in the marketplace. Focusing on these issues, rather than on "customer satisfaction," will bridge the gap between what the customers actually receive from the seller and what they really desire to receive.

"It's not my job, man!"

David Goldsmith, author of *Understanding the Real Reason Customers Buy*, talks about passing the buck in business. I love reading it because I have experienced these things so often as a consumer. Just think how many times you have heard these excuses:

- "That's not my area, you need to see Phyliss."
- "I don't know anything about that—you need to call Jim tomorrow."
- "We don't sell those, and I don't know where you can get them."

Passing the buck is part of the American landscape. It is also a factor in the destruction of many businesses. It's completely unacceptable yet it's so incredibly common in every area of commerce today.

Goldsmith points out that everything we do (or don't do) impacts the customer. The way you walk, talk, smile, or help out can mean hundreds, thousands, hundreds of thousands, even millions in sales...or losses. The adage that the purpose of being in business is not to make a profit...but to make and keep a customer is more profound today than ever before. Again, it's not about price or specific product value. It's all about attitude and service.

When customers are shopping for a specific item, they stop looking once they locate someone who really shows concern in helping them. If the item costs more than it does at the other place, who cares? What matters is that people feel cared for, because this is worth more than anything.

Because caring is so critical, Goldsmith stresses being "*response-able.*" Being response-able means responding to the customer and being able to exceed their needs. We all acknowledge that most of us feel mild to moderate contempt in our everyday dealings with businesses. Maybe it's the lack of a smile from the restaurant owner who sells us coffee in the morning or the indifferent tone from a supplier. When businesses adopt an extreme customer service attitude, things change dramatically.

In his desire to make a difference and bring his passion and knowledge to business owners and corporations, David Goldsmith founded CustomerEdge, a consulting firm that focuses on corporate restructuring through improved customer care. He also publishes *Daily Service*, a customer service periodical, and an e-mail newsletter which is read daily by subscribers around the world. (For more information about the CustomerEdge company and the publications, send e-mail to: info@customeredge.com.)

Training your people to love customers

If you look at statistics, there are three types of customer service people/salespeople:

1. **Underachievers:** 15 percent of the workforce falls into this category. Underachievers will respond that, "it's not my job." They are difficult to train and very easy to recognize. This group ideally should be eliminated from your organization because you will likely suffer at their hands—especially if they come in contact with your customers.
2. **Safe-zoners:** 70 percent of all people in the workforce are in this nice, easy, and safe category. They're not likely to offend your customers but they won't excite them either. They're trainable and you can motivate them, but it's not easy. The reason they're safe-zoners is that they've never been pushed to perform...that's your job.
3. **Overachievers:** 15 percent of the working population falls into this enviable category. They're a glorious bunch of self-starters who truly want to succeed in whatever they do, and they usually do succeed. They're easier to recognize than the safe zoners because they are the first ones in line, the first ones to seize the moment with a customer, the first to ask questions, and the first to offer answers. Finding them is not easy because once they're discovered, they're gobbled up by anyone and everyone.

If we look at our customer service team, we first have to look at the carrot that is suspended on the stick in front of them. Even a carrot that would choke a giant bunny wouldn't budge the underachiever. So, for the moment, let's discount this group and move on. Safe-zoners have some potential to become players in your organization if they are trained and motivated properly. The ideal customer service employee is that person who recognizes that their own success is tied to the success of the relationship with the customer. Safe-zoners need to be educated to excel beyond the boundaries they normally feel secure within.

Just saying yes defuses the fastest burning fuse

If you want to win people over, just say yes! Simply agreeing with them may not be factually right...but in business it's more important to be smart than to be right.

We want our employees to agree with their customers. When the customer returns a dress because it's ripped, she has the receipt, and it indicates that the dress was purchased during the past week, would you want to argue over how the dress ripped? Clearly the seam opened. You have two options...to win or to lose. Winning requires you to be as enthusiastic in handling the refund, exchange, or repair as you were in handling the sale (it's up to the customer). The other option includes questioning the customer about the tear and making the resolution difficult, embarrassing, or tense. You lose if you choose any of these options.

Don't be fooled by the uncombed hair...

Charlie Adler, one of my first clients, looked disheveled the first time I met him. When I saw him, I thought he was a low-level worker, not the president and founder of two very successful firms. Charlie wore a shirt that was so wrinkled I couldn't believe it when he was introduced to me as the boss. I later discovered that the wrinkled shirt was imported Italian silk and cost $300. Interesting enough, my reaction to Charlie changed dramatically when I learned that this "wrinkled" look was fashionable for the rich at the time. When Charlie stepped into his $80,000 Mercedes, my interest in him became even more intensified! Why did I experience a one hundred eighty degree turn in my interest in him, and more importantly, in my treatment and attitude toward him? Social conditioning, that's why.

Remember Julia Roberts in *Pretty Woman*? She goes shopping in Beverly Hills in her street attire and is rebuffed by the employee of a fancy store. Then, after she hooks up with Richard Gere and returns to the same store dressed to kill, carrying packages from every boutique in the area, she is treated like royalty. She then reminds them of the previous experience when she appeared to be just a plain old customer.

Do we treat people differently based upon appearance? Absolutely. Our perceptions dictate our behavior to a large degree. Studies have indicated that good looking people are waited on first, fastest, and best by employees. Are shopkeepers and business owners prejudiced? Of course they are. Businesses put the energy where they believe there's the greatest return...and appearance dictates potential return.

Rich people receive better service than everyone else. That's a fact. The reason is that they represent more potential to the business owner. However, there are some wonderful exceptions. A few years ago, Geraldo Rivera and his wife, C.C., came into Ray's Restaurant in New Jersey. My party had just been seated in this funky cafe in a marina.

Ray is about 60 years old and is a character. Nothing in the restaurant matches, the floors and tables are uneven, the ceiling fans are noisy—you know, really shabby, but chic nonetheless. But, the place had a great reputation that crossed all economic boundaries. They made great pasta, lobster, seafood...you name it. Fisherman, clammers, locals, and local celebrities frequent the place.

When Geraldo walked in with his wife and another couple, I expected Ray to greet them with more enthusiasm than he greeted me and everyone else. Instead, he nodded hello, shook hands quickly, and told them it would be about an hour wait. They asked if they could sit in their car until a table was ready. Ray took his cellular number and told them he'd call them when they could be seated. I asked Geraldo if he often enjoyed more obvious benefits to his celebrity. To his credit, he said he was happy to be treated the same as everyone else...as it should be.

This, however is a complete anomaly in our society today. For the most part, businesses respond differently to people like Geraldo. Anne Obarski recently wrote about this happening in customer service. The article, "Clothes Might Make the Man but Clothes Do Not Make a Customer" in *Retail Store News* spoke of an incident where a secret shopper employed by Anne was asked to shop in a store that carried a line of women's suits. The employee was thrilled to shop the store because she had done so previously, though not as a secret shopper. She loved the store and was excited about the assignment. Interestingly enough, on this occasion, she was heading to the store from her home. On all the other occasions, she would stop at this store on her way from work. However, on this occasion, she was very dressed down. She was also sporting a cast on her foot, and she had to wear very casual pants to leave room for the broken foot. Pam was excited when she entered the store to see her favorite salesperson, who had always been helpful. This time, the associate looked the other way, never acknowledging that she was in the store. None of the other salespeople acknowledged her either.

Pam recognized that the difference in her appearance caused a difference in their attitude and behavior. She never returned to that store as a customer.

Statistics show that three out of four customers leave a business environment because of inattentive, impolite customer service or rude sales associates. Statistically, unhappy customers will tell between 10 and 20 other people about their bad experience. It's also interesting to remember that most customers will never express their discontent...they'll simply stop doing business with you.

Chapter 9

Ask a Futurist Where Customers Are Headed!

They are everywhere. There's no escape from them in most of the businesses that you frequent today. For example, how often have you ever heard the following phrases?

- All sales are final.
- Restrooms are for customers only.
- Refunds are given as store credit only!
- All returns must be accompanied by a receipt.
- Exchanges cannot be made after 30 days.
- Sale does not include previously discounted items.

There are many more, there just isn't enough room to print them all. Futurists (marketing scientists who study future trends, technologies, and business applications) are truly upset by our "customer unfriendly" past. The American Society of Quality Service is disturbed by the trend away from good service. Customers are completely dismayed.

Watts Wacker, futurist and consumer research guru, has told us that there are no untouched customers. All customers come to all businesses with a certain degree of baggage. Businesses have to understand the customer's feelings in order to serve them well.

Wacker has indicated the top five "megatrends" which will illustrate how schizophrenic our society is because of the contradictions. In examining these trends, it's important for us to interpret how they affect the way in which we do business and what's really important to customers today. Let's review the top five megatrends that are evolving today:

1. Personal safety.
2. Gender equity.
3. A search for community.
4. Physical fitness and well-being.
5. Respect for experience.

Personal safety

Consumers want to be safe, to feel safe, and to deal with companies that produce safe products. Safety is an issue that covers the integrity of the product, the credibility of the company, the way in which employees treat customers, and the policies that make people feel good about their transactions. It makes sense. We, as consumers, need to feel safe about whom we do business with. We need to know that the rocking chair won't collapse while we're cradling a baby in our arms. We need to feel secure that the sleep aid won't kill us or that the canned peas won't cause stomach ailments or the car won't take off on its own or the airlines won't overlook safety features in an effort to create economies. We need and want to feel safe. It's an understandable and somewhat obvious trend.

Gender equity

No one wants to do business with companies that treat women unfairly (and, for that matter, anyone else). More and more women will be taking over leadership roles in our society...from the companies we do business with to the political offices locally and nationally. What's amazing to me about businesses today is that while women are emerging in business, they still represent the vast minority of management personnel.

This trend isn't only about women, though. It's about equity in general. Companies whose human resources do not reflect our culture, society, community, or customer base are doing both themselves and the customer a great disservice. Many large and small businesses alike pay little or no attention to the issue of equity in the workforce. Can you imagine owning a small Hispanic cheese company where all the salespeople are Germans? How about a niche market African grocery supplier who doesn't employ one African American? It's truly preposterous...but it's the norm rather than the exception. The trend toward equity means that businesses that do not have a proactive program regarding this issue will be out of business.

A search for community

As a trend, community relates to the notion that we all want to feel as though we belong to the businesses we do business with. It's a significant concept because extreme customer service is based upon the premise that we need to get closer to the customer and to interact in more meaningful ways—through personal contact, continuous mail contact, e-mail, Web contact, phone contact, and social contact. The need for a sense of community is what propelled Ben & Jerry's to stardom and is what is fostering the growth of many niche market companies who see themselves as part of the local, regional and national community. Many include the international community as part of their domain.

Physical fitness and well-being

As a trend, physical fitness has been evolving during the past decade. The industries that have benefitted greatly include home fitness equipment, vitamin and mineral supplements, and holistic and alternative health care. Consciousness has been raised about all of the different aspects of maintaining one's health as well as practicing preventive medicine.

Well-being also includes emotional health, and the practice of meditation is growing. Zen philosophy has never been more popular or widely read. The Dalai Lama is now known in America and around the world. The idea that we're taking better care of ourselves needs to be woven into our thinking when we think about how well we need to take care of each other.

Respect for experience

Respect for experience begins with the notion that all consumers want to believe that the people who sell them stuff know what they're selling. Simply stated, if you're going to sell a product or service, sell it well. You need to know *everything* there is to know about your product or service. The customer wants to deal with an expert in every facet of their life...from healthcare to health food.

When I shopped for outdoor furnishings recently, I went to a large store known for its selection. I assumed that, along with this abundance of inventory, there would be an abundance of information. However, each question that I asked was answered by handing me the literature pertaining to that particular manufacturer. I left and sought out a small store with fewer choices, but a knowledgeable salesperson. I probably paid more, but I got much more. I was educated enough to make an informed buying decision.

Experts are people who care enough about their product or service to understand it completely. People care about that. We respect experience, not for its own sake but rather for the fact that experience typically shows expert behavior based on a history in that business. When people come to me for customer service and marketing consulting, they do so because I've spent more than 25 years doing what I do well. There's experience and tangible results to point to...yet, most automobile dealerships employ neophytes, most banks employ clerks to handle customers, most airlines never, ever create "experts" in customer relations, and most businesses today don't take the time or money to cultivate and expert population of staff members.

6 fastest "changing" megatrends

Now that we've established the groundwork for the top five megatrends, here's a list of the six fastest "changing" megatrends, according to Watts Wacker. Look for the schizophrenic nature of how people respond.

1. Personal safety.
2. Flirting with danger.
3. Brand image.

4. Winning.
5. Romanticism.
6. Privacy.

Flirting with danger

On the one hand, the population is telling us that personal safety is a top megatrend, yet in response to the fastest changing trends, what happens? We want danger in our lives!

We're all aging. Many of us are turning 50...or older. We have unmet expectations and we want immediate gratification. It's why we are the most demanding customers out there...and we want to flirt with danger so that we can feel as though we're still young enough to get the thrills we used to.

Harley Davidson has a waiting list for their motorcycles, and guess who's waiting? Baby boomers—doctors, lawyers, CEOs, accountants, plumbers, and construction workers (not kids with leather jackets). Flirtation with danger provides the necessary balance in our life...and it's important to understand who the customer is and what he or she wants if we want to outservice the competitors. Bungee jumping, extreme sports, safaris, white water rafting, adventure travel of every conceivable kind, parachuting out of small planes, rock climbing...these are the industries and issues that consumers want to take part in.

Brand imaging

Brand imaging has never been as powerful a selling force as it is today. Customers are saying that they believe in brands because they have a sense of higher expectations when they choose a brand that has communicated its worth to them. It makes perfect sense.

Branding sends an unmistakable message of quality to the customer. It's why extreme customer service is the most effective tool in branding today. Consumers have been raised on brands they trust and like brands to be consistent—if not downright exciting. The customer prefers the feeling of confidence they get from a branded product to the false security of saving a little money. The trend is for broader branding in our business culture.

Small business branding is exploding. Think about it: In your own community, there is a pizzeria brand, an insurance agent brand, a host of bank brands, a deli brand, a bunch of supermarket brands, a bagel shop brand, a dry cleaner brand, and so forth. Every small business has brand potential within the market or community they serve, and people love the idea that they will get consistent behavior and products from the "brands" in their lives. Branding behavior is what made Nordstrom great. It's clearly what can make you great as well. Extreme customer service is completely brandable, regardless of what business you're in. You begin by identifying a singular principle that can represent you as a brand. For example, if you're in the construction business and build decks, then you should guarantee timetables, performance, and estimates. Look to issues that are weak in your industry and overcome them with an extreme customer service agenda that will break through the clutter and become your brand image. But if you say it, you have to do it!

Winning

We all want to win in our business relationships. It implies that the consumer doesn't feel as though he or she is winning in business, career, or relationships. We want the proverbial win/win situation and extreme customer service actually creates an imbalance in the business arena by suggesting that we'll do anything for the customer. The customer should feel as though they're close to taking advantage of the business—much in the way that I still feel that I underpaid for that incredible lunch that came with all the complimentary extras. So, if we create a win/win situation, the customer feels much better and spends more.

Romancing the customer

Romanticism is not only a "changing" trend, it is also a welcome one. It counters cynicism and offers hope to skeptics. Romanticism is about "relating" to one another. It does not imply physical intimacy, but rather a notion of caring and trust. Romancing the customer is about treating them the way you would an audience member if you were appearing on stage in a play. An example of this would include a poetic reading of Elizabethan verse, accompanied by harp and flute sounds while you were on hold, rather than the standard elevator music. Such a company is looking to romance you, while you anticipate your party picking up the phone.

Privacy

Privacy has become a greater issue recently. The Internet poses privacy issues, the Web can undermine anonymity, the use of credit cards over the phone can cause fraud, ATM machines, health insurance claims—even a preferred customer card from your local supermarket can invade your privacy. We want to ensure our customers that we protect their privacy and that, in our dealings with them, we will keep all information secure. It's a strong selling proposition. Tell your customers that you don't share information, buying behavior, or anything pertaining to their relationship with you. Extreme customer service acknowledges the intimacy of the exchange and the need to keep the relationship proprietary.

Watch these 5 growing trends!

In a 1996 study by Yankelovich, the following issues were offered as compelling trends heading into the new millennium:

1. Creativity.
2. Customizing.
3. A nonhypocritical attitude.
4. Religion.
5. Hedonism.

Creativity

Creativity is emerging as a concept in business, as well as life. It is the business owner's responsibility to take creative control and to develop and rethink the way customers can become excited. By raising the noise level with creative imagery, messages, and notions, we attract attention to ourselves and draw attention away from our competitors. Sometimes it's as simple as a guarantee, a customer-appreciation theme or program, or an eclectic mix of these as I've discussed in previous chapters. To understand creativity, one must look at what is done daily and stretch each aspect of it in order to expand horizons and "create" new policies, procedures, plans, activities, and communications.

Customizing

The customizing process brings businesses much closer to the customer by focusing on their specific needs and passions. For example, the jeweler who illustrates his customized approach to jewelry runs commercials that show him smashing rubber jewelry molds with a mallet to show his desire to design products for the individual. This same jeweler ran a print advertisement that I wrote for him. The headline was: "Three things you never want to see at a dinner party: Your dress on someone else, your bracelet on someone else, or your husband on someone else."

The copy showed off his ability to create a look that is not available anywhere else. Of course, an irreverent tone was used to dramatize, tease, and humor the customer...and clearly it can only be run in markets where the risk of offense is minimal.

A nonhypocritical attitude

The hatred of hypocrisy came through loud and clear. Most people want equity, not hypocritical behavior. That's why brokerage companies, insurance companies, and Fortune 500 corporations, among others, have been under attack in recent years for gender bias, age discrimination, or sexual harassment. Simply stated, customers won't do business with you if you're hypocritical. Your business culture must reflect an attitude of inclusion and tolerance or get ready to coast into oblivion.

Religion

Never before in the history of television has there been such an abundance of shows about angels, God, religion, or families struggling through a variety of spiritual crises. Religious affiliation and connections are up and, depending upon the market you're in, you're expected to behave in a way that is appropriate to moral, ethical, and religious doctrine.

Hedonism

Are you ready for this...religious thought is a growing trend but hedonism is as well. The research ironically includes both as responses from consumers. What this says is that the buying public wants to remain grounded in principles, yet wants to explore an adventurous side of themselves as well. However, this has to be put in perspective. Baby boomers are the largest category of respondents to the consumer research because they're the largest demographic group. Baby boomers are turning back to old traditions, but they are also running as fast as they can into excess because they're aging and need to feel alive. Amazingly, hedonistic behavior is up, yet hedonistic values are down.

You have 3 customers

What does all of this mean? It means that you need to understand what people are thinking and where they're trending in order to excite and delight them in business. To this point, let's look at your customers relative to their categories of life and their respective values.

- **Matures:** I call this the "'Whoa' Is Me Generation," born from 1909 to 1945.
- **Boomers:** The "Me Generation," born from 1946 to 1964.
- **Gen Xers:** The "Why Me Generation," born from 1965 to 1984.

Of course, there are people who were born from 1984 to the present, but for purposes of business categories, we'll leave the "Generation Y" alone for the time being. They are great consumers, but they have no income—only influence.

Matures

Matures have a constrained set of expectations and traditional values, are financially and socially conservative, and are slow to embrace new ideas. We need to market to them carefully because they are very demanding and forthright. The extreme customer service approach with matures is to bend over backwards to please them. They are enormously vocal and have more discretionary income than ever before in history.

Obviously we want to please all our customers, but matures feel that by virtue of their seniority in our society they should be catered to...and I don't disagree.

Boomers

Boomers are the largest demographic block with more discretionary dollars than any other group in our country. They were born to prosperity and have a strong need for instant gratification. Boomers also have a sense of entitlement with unmet expectations. Many industries have resulted from this demographic group that didn't exist or exist to the same degree with previous generations.

Adventure travel, one-price car dealerships, plastic surgery, running and walking shoes, cosmetics for men, environmentally sound products, meal delivery services, massage therapy, bottled water, personal trainers, exercise clubs, cellular phones, books on tape, and many more. The mere size of the market has caused baby boomers to become a spoiled generation. They not only need service, they will judge their commitment to a business based upon how well they're treated.

Gen Xers

Generation X is more similar to the matures than they are to their own parents. They're savvy, hard working, and look like boomers of 20 years ago. They're also very wary as to where they stand in society and are uncertain about their economic future. They are an emerging market and for many industries, they represent future prosperity. They need care and attention and, while they're more cynical about service, they're like sponges when they receive positive energy from businesses. They're also incredibly brand loyal if they are treated well.

Boomers are your biggest block of customers—treat them well!

Boomers want things their way...and at more than 40 percent of consumer demand, it behooves you to understand how to woo them. Rich Kizer and Georganne Bender, authors of *The Power Consumers,* analyzed boomers and illustrate just how powerful they are to businesses today. From 1946 to 1964, 76 million babies were born. Nothing in our society has been the same since.

The boomer was the first to break long-held societal rules, say the authors. Boomers question everything. As consumers, they won't accept foolish statements such as, "we're out of stock" or "we'll have to order it for you." Instant gratification is necessary to make them fall in love with you. If you're not willing to cater to their considerable whims, perhaps you should rethink who you want as your customer.

Statistically, the size of this market is staggering, so pay attention to every nuance of extreme customer service as it pertains to keeping your boomer customers loyal. There are 11,000 boomers turning 50 every day. The fact is that if the AARP were to send a mailing out every eight seconds, they still couldn't keep up.

Aging is a difficult part of their lives...which is why this generation has given rise to so many health and fitness products and services designed to put off the inevitable wrinkles.

They are in the midst of what we call the "sandwich cycle." They are caught between college-aged children and elderly parents. The economic impact of this life situation causes them to seriously think about who they buy from. This is important: Baby boomers (who represent approximately 60 percent or more of your customer base) constantly complain about time poverty. They are besieged by economic issues like large mortgages, golf club memberships, and all the accoutrements that they fed themselves during the enormous prosperity of the 1980s.

Stress is a major complaint for baby boomers as well. They realize that they will probably be working for most of their lives and time is something this generation desires more than anything else. They want to do business with businesses who demonstrate a desire to excite and delight.

Keep them happy, and they will come

The singule most critical issue in gaining and keeping baby boomers as customers is through extreme customer service. Creativity is so important that I cannot stress the fact that you simply can't over-service this market. Look at ways of making their lives easier...with conveniences such as delivery services, value added components to the sale, promises that you can keep...all the over-the-line issues that will distinguish you as a business willing to please, at any cost!

The question you should be asking isn't "how can I help you?"—it's "what can I possibly do to make your life easier?" Boomers want your undivided attention and if they can't get it from you, they'll find it elsewhere.

Gary Riccardi is cleaning up!

Gary Riccardi owns three dry cleaning stores in suburban towns. He is a baby boomer himself: He is 48 years old and married, with two children. Ten years ago, he had one store and was struggling to reach his financial goals. He asked himself what he would find important as a consumer dealing with a dry cleaning establishment. There were a host of ideas that were generated from his wife, friends, and family. He finally compiled a list and developed his business from it. After all of his changes, he was making approximately half of a million dollars per year...and driving a Rolls Royce.

His first change involved pickup and delivery, but that wasn't particularly unique. Secondly, since most of his customers dropped their clothes off on the way to work (between 7 a.m. and 9 a.m.) he made sure that there were pots of gourmet-blend coffee (decaf, regular, and flavored) in the store. Further, he had prewrapped bagels with cream cheese or butter, croissants, muffins and cookies for his customers. At first, they were hesitant to take the free food (especially since his store shared a strip center with a coffee shop). After a while, his customers gave in to Gary's generosity and appreciated the extra thoughtfulness bestowed upon them.

Gary did something else for his boomer customers. He offered his customers the opportunity to have their shoes professionally polished for free. Many of his customers dropped shoes off regularly with their cleaning orders...and Gary used his equipment to buff and polish the shoes, returning them to the customer like new. He figured that the increased cleaning volume paid for the shoe polishing equipment in less then four months.

The amazing thing about extreme customer service is that as soon as it begins to dominate a community or market, competition always attempts to keep up. In Gary's case, not only was he first, he was the best. Aside from these innovative gestures of appreciation for the customer, Gary's staff knew the credo of the company: Just say yes to anything they ask. If a customer wants to wind their way through the maze of equipment to use the restroom, of course they may. If a customer wants a shirt done while they wait, they can get it for a price. If a customer complains about a stain that didn't come out, they'll reclean the garment and if it still doesn't come out, they'll offer a certificate for three free cleanings. Does all this cost Gary money? Of course it does. His food costs, polishing costs, free cleaning costs, and delivery costs all add up...but the bottom line is they add up to 38 percent more volume than he did before and his business is growing all the time.

Custom orders, fast deliveries, gift wrapping, shipping, phone orders, personal shopping, 20-minute callbacks, guaranteed estimates in one day...the creative list is endless. But these options are what businesses need to be thinking about when they think about creating more volume through baby boomers.

Kizer and Bender tell us to "think of what conveniences a time-starved customer needs, and add them to the list of services you already offer. Flexibility is critical when marketing to your largest customer base, the boomer!"

Romancing the boomer

We've just spoken about romanticism as an emerging trend. Romancing the baby boomer isn't easy, but it is worthwhile. Making them love you begins with sincerity and true eagerness to please. Remember that the services described in Gary Riccardi's business dramatically decrease sensitivity to price. In Riccardi's case, he's competitively priced, but his customers stopped asking about the cost of cleaning a tie a long time ago.

Boomers want a relationship with you...in fact they search desperately to fill their lives with "suppliers" to suit their needs and lifestyles. Customization includes varying any product, service, or program that will please their sensibilities.

Personal marketing to the boomer can be in the form of a handwritten note, an invitation—anything. It should always communicate on a one-to-one basis with an emphasis on the customer, and not on yourself. As I have stated before in *Start Up Marketing*, there's no **me** in marketing. Well, it isn't in extreme customer service either. Inviting your customer to an open house or a special event based upon their specific interests can be an amazing method of getting them to love you.

I asked Gary Ricardi what he knew about his customers. He replied that he knew very little. I asked him if he knows what kind of clothes they wear—and perhaps even the kind of work they do while talking with them during the early morning hours. After he said that he did, I suggested that he create a database that includes whatever information he has about the customer. I also suggested that he ask the customer to fill out a short survey in order to receive special promotions and mailings.

He eventually told me how many of his customers brought in riding outfits to get cleaned because two of his three stores were near many stables. I thought this was a wonderful opportunity to take advantage of the information we had. Why not direct some extreme customer service to these customers? Gary then had riding scarves monogrammed with the initials of the some 60 or so customers who had been bringing in riding-related apparel for cleaning. It cost him $12 per scarf plus another $1.50 for each box with his logo on a silver sticker that was stuck on the top of each box. His expense was approximately $800. He eventually mailed or personally handed out each of the 60 scarves within a two month period. He received phone calls, notes, and personal thanks from the customers who immediately began dealing with him on a more intimate basis. The frequency of those customers to his store rose by 25 percent. Did these customers suddenly have an increase in their wardrobes? Probably not. But their relationship with him prompted them to think about his business and their dry cleaning needs more frequently.

By the way, Gary is evolving his extreme customer service philosophy onto the Internet as well. He e-mails willing customers specials. He even sends notes reminding them to pick up their cleaning or call for delivery. He also uses e-mail to thank them for their business and is moving toward a complete system of communicating by e-mail on a regular basis.

Extreme customer service as a branding tool can be quickly illustrated by an example given by Jack Trout and Al Ries in *The 22 Immutable Laws of Marketing*. They list a few brands and the focus point for each one. Here's the list:

- Crest: cavities.
- Mercedes: engineering.
- BMW: driving.
- Volvo: safety.
- Domino's: home delivery.
- Pepsi Cola: youth.
- Nordstrom: service.

What if you could own a great reputation for service, while you add on other issues that will focus you further? Wouldn't that be the most exciting goal you have in your quest to increase your wealth? The futurists have identified what people say they want, how they act, and the inconsistencies. We need to extrapolate from this information the most exploitable issues of our business. Nordstrom owns service. Everyone knows they have great quality, selection, and value...but they *own* service. Your goal is to own service in your marketplace by doing just that. Then, reflecting back on the futurists' research, you will own the market share. That's where the majority of customers are today...and that's what will get you where you want to go.

Chapter 10

Mind Your Own Business

There are no rules in business—only guidelines. If you look past authority, prerequisites, and preconceptions, you force originality. If your business closes at 6 p.m. and a customer shows up at 6:30 while you're cleaning the floors, the question is, "do you open the doors?" What's your answer, "I've put in a full day, I'm tired, let 'em come back tomorrow!" Or, "My purpose is to serve the customer's needs, I'll fly open the doors and invite them in!"

It's your choice and the tools are within you. It all depends upon your agenda. If you truly invest in the power of extreme customer service, then you need to keep a policy statement regarding these issues in your pocket at all times. When in doubt, simply refer to your policy statement and act accordingly. Your entire team should keep this in their pockets as well.

And, speaking of your people, ask each of them what the purpose of the company is. Then ask them what strategy can be used in accomplishing the purpose of the company. We don't need to call it a "mission" or a "vision," just a "purpose." Analyze their answers and teach accordingly.

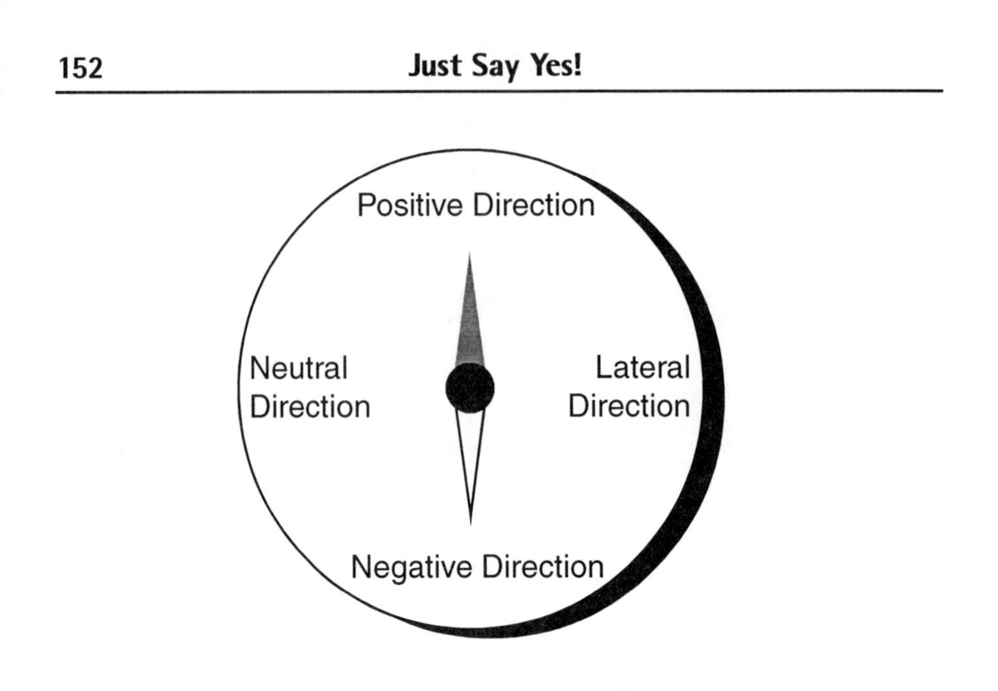

Let your business compass direct you

Bring out your business compass. You can see it above. Teach competency to your team by showing them that when you go off course, even by one degree, you will not reach your destination. If they speak indifferently, the company position is at jeopardy, and its direction is changed. If any employee forgets the company credo, even without offending the customer, they have only achieved mediocrity. If they simply do their job and nothing more, they have made a move which gets them and the company nowhere. If they are rude, indifferent, not accommodating, or challenging, they have spoiled the chart and negativity ensues. Remember there's a big difference between a mission/vision statement and your management style. Your purpose is to empower; your style is to ensure compliance!

Take your people on a fire walk

Firewalkers learn to walk on red hot embers without pain or injury. They do so by focusing their attention on a singular, well-defined issue that distracts and protects them. When employees enter your business they're on a fire walk, one that cannot permit distraction.

You can draw people to your business by creating *perceptions* that must become *realities* when they give money for products or services.

Advertising can change commonly held beliefs if done with credibility, authenticity, and reality.

Here's what each and every one of your team members must be educated and empowered to do. They must:

- Create demand in their exchange with the customer by offering a risk-reduced opportunity.
- Illustrate brand differentiation by pointing to the numerous value-added components of your business purpose.
- Ensure follow-through on orders, service, guarantees, information, rebates, and so forth.
- Provide all the necessary data the customer needs to ensure the successful use of the service or product.
- Make it personal.

Surveys reveal that the most effective use of advertising relates to the issue of guarantees and service warranties. By service, we mean both physical and psychological service. FedEx will track your shipment and provide valuable customer follow-through, but their service philosophy is what positions them in the marketplace and communicates their business purpose: "When it absolutely, positively has to be there overnight" was the concept that built their business. What's your concept?

Remember, your employees are also your customers. Excite them and they will excite others...but they need the purpose. The purpose is your business. Define each and every aspect of your business, including your personal goals in evolving the business forward. Start living your purpose and they will too.

Amazingly, in business today, we tend to reward business...so why not reward innovation? For every idea that a team member offers, a reward should be offered...an extra half hour for lunch for a mediocre idea; a day off for a good idea; an extra week's pay for a brilliant idea. Remember, recognition is still the number one motivator, so recognize trying as well as performance.

Change isn't easy

Here's a good exercise. Have your employees fold their arms in front of them. Now, simply ask them to reverse their arms. It's very difficult, uncomfortable—even awkward. It shows that change is uncomfortable and most people do resist discomfort. It may not be easy for employees to change their behavior and smile all the time or reach out to a customer when they're tired or frustrated. Change isn't a negotiable item, though. If they aren't naturally inclined to follow your purpose, they must change or perish. It's that simple.

Statistically, change occurs in three days of training. However, the maximum you should commit to training an employee to change is 21 days. Pain, pleasure, and perception all cause change. When people reach awareness of your plan, they change. However, if they fall into a rut, they are unconsciously incompetent. If they resist change, they become consciously incompetent. When we make a commitment to change, we become consciously competent.

You must have a zero tolerance policy toward the customer service portion of your business. Most businesses need to change to adopt an extreme customer service posture, and most business owners must change as well. If they are not willing to change, you may not want them in your organization.

Tell your people that you don't have all the answers, unless you know their questions. You need to exhaust their questions with answers and they need to understand your answers before they can change. Motorola Corporation provides a minimum of 40 hours of training per employee per year. They ask questions, provide answers, and review performance.

Total Quality Management teaches us that the aim of the team leader (manager or owner) should be to institute leadership. In and of itself, this is not very profound. Although this is common sense, it's enormously significant. The aim of leadership is to help people and technology to do a better job. The crisis in customer service today is in the lack of supervision of the team as well as those responsible for product quality and follow-through. The idea that the business owner should drive fear out of the workplace is part of the leadership role.

In fact, the word "fear" has created a contemporary acronym within itself: **F**alse **E**vidence **A**ppearing **R**eal. When workers are afraid, they're usually prompted by "owner-attitude" which evokes insecurity. It's important that your people recognize that they have the ability (indeed the responsibility) to speak out in order to contribute to improving methods of doing business. When you break down barriers between owners, workers, and departments, creating an inclusive, cohesive "contact" system between all employees, then the whole is enhanced.

The idea that you should impose absolutes in the workplace is dangerous. By telling people that you will not tolerate any deviations from your system creates adversarial relationships. The only zero tolerance policy worth adopting and keeping pertains to attitude, not product variations, features or benefits. The difference between a quota and an incentive is the difference between a dictatorship and a capitalist regime. Also, eliminate management by objective. Eliminate management by the numbers and numerical musts...substitute leadership and creative methods of moving people to perform. This can be accomplished by instituting a vigorous program of education and self-improvement which can only be done by top management. The transformation of a work-force into a team is the move from customer management to extreme customer service.

Let's look at an Asian system of quality leadership, customer service and planning. You should establish these goals with your team:

- **Quality:** Raising expectations so standards are set, not met.
- **Quantity:** The productivity of each team member depends upon an arrangement, setting objectives that apply to all members of the company.
- **Cost:** Realistic pricing of products and services is an imperative to compete in the marketplace.
- **Timeliness:** Meeting and exceeding the customers' time-frame is a commitment that has little room for error.

SMART is a good place to start

I mentioned the following acronym in my first book. However, I believe that it is worth mentioning again, as we look at extreme customer service from the top down:

S **Specific:** Be clear with your team. Tell them what the collective goals are and ask for their participation, as well as their recommendations.

M **Measurable:** Quantify the goals. Place real numbers, profits, and growth figures into the equation so that each team member recognizes that what they do affects the measurable portion of your business.

A **Agreed-upon:** Mutual confirmation of the business goals and framework helps accomplish the goals by including the entire company in the "agreed upon" principles.

R **Realistic:** Do not create "pie-in-the-sky" aspirations that cannot possibly be met. Assess the reality of everything you put on the table so that the team can understand clearly what it will take to effect the change that's been put in motion.

T **Time frame:** Establish "settings" for accomplishing tasks. Create timed guidelines rather than deadlines. Deadlines are fixed and intimidating, Motivating people to timed guidelines is easier to accomplish, and creates less stress and anxiety.

Customer ID

"Participation is something the top orders the middle to do with the bottom."

—Rosabeth Moss Kanter

The process continues by what I call "Customer ID." Unlike Caller ID, Customer ID exposes the identity of the customers to the team. In order to create an extreme customer service posture, a portrait of the customer must be created in order for everyone to understand exactly who the most valued resource of the business is.

Next, pinpoint the needs of your customers. When it comes to selling your product or service, be an educator, not a predator. Only create a system that sells based upon who the customer is as well as what they want and need. Often, businesses disregard the customer and focus on the product—attempting to fit the customer to the product. This is suicide for your business.

Now, we need to create product features and benefits that match those needs and wants. Customizing comes into play. We can design a product or service that suits the needs of the customer even if it doesn't fit our own line. Extreme customer service marketing begins by identifying customized needs (remember *customer* comes from *custom*) and changing our own product line or service to meet those needs.

Japanese electronics manufacturers create products based upon what the customer dictates—not what operational issues dictate. Remember the bagel store who met the needs of his customers by increasing the size of bagels for sandwiches and creating no-hole bagels? His production changed in order to please the customer. This is a very important part of extreme customer service. We not only need to just say yes to the customer verbally...we need to just say yes to the customer relative to the product or service itself. When we augment a product or enhance a service based upon the needs of the user, we are employing a "just say yes" philosophy of extreme customer service.

Now that you've agreed to change your business in terms of products and services, you need to implement methods for producing those products. This means that you need to employ integrity, production, creativity, and a whole lot of energy into ensuring that the "customer-produced" products are sound. Lastly, stay abreast of the quality process and continually inform all personnel.

You are destined to fail if...

- All employees are not involved in defining the company or at least participating in the process.
- Your focus is constantly on cutting costs and not the extreme service of the customer.
- People in your organization are unwilling to change.
- Problem-solving teams are not established.
- Suggested changes or ideas from workers are ignored.
- Employees are not rewarded for giving exceptional service to customers.
- Information and ideas regarding any and all successful customer service experiences are not shared with everyone.
- The quality effort is not clearly defined through the use of examples. If it is deemed just another buzzword, it will be perceived as another attempt by management to get more work out of workers.
- Upper-level management does not stay committed and involved in the entire extreme customer service process every day.

You cannot afford bad impressions

If there are any members of your staff who have ever said, "We tried something like that before and it didn't work," remove them

Quality Communication: Do's and Don'ts

Avoid these types of responses:

"That will never work."

"We tried that once."

"That's not the way we do things around here."

"It's too costly."

"The boss doesn't believe in that."

"That's too radical an idea."

"You don't understand our business."

Instead, use these:

"What is your opnion?"

"What might we be forgetting or overlooking?"

"Give me more details."

"Could you please put some of those thoughts in writing?"

"Please expand on that concept."

"Let's share that with the others."

"That may very well improve the process."

immediately from your business or begin an intensive training program to alter the way they think. If you don't, they will undoubtedly infect the entire organization.

Because people on average will talk about a negative experience four times more often than a positive one, major attrition will occur in your business if you create even a few negative impressions. You simply cannot afford to do that.

Philosophically (according to TQM), the definition of a customer is someone who is affected by the vision and goals of our quality program. In extreme customer service, we go beyond that statement: "A customer is someone who is profoundly moved by the vision and experience of our program...moved to tell others enthusiastically!"

Jan Carzon, President of SAS Airlines, wrote in a 1999 *New York Times* article that the "moment of truth" occurs when a customer walks away with one of four feelings: negative, indifferent, positive, or magical. The idea that each and every member of the organization affects customer attitude toward the company is profound.

An electric utility company conducted a quality survey. Only 25 percent of the employees considered themselves to have customers. Every single person in your organization (including the maintenance staff) has customers. Every single person in your organization can affect your customers' perceptions of you. The question we need to ask is this: "Is your organization customer-driven or procedure-driven?" If the task is what drives the employees, then retrain the employees to recognize that procedures are only part of the process to achieve a delightful experience for the customer.

The baker who spends his time reading trade journals on better baking needs to recognize that, even though he's in the backroom baking, the procedures don't drive the business. He needs to be a great baker and an even greater practitioner of extreme customer service. He needs to get out of the back room like any chef in any restaurant and meet his public. Procedures are there only to delight customers with superb products or services...not as a means to an end.

Extreme customer service creativity can be exercised when we understand what drives the customer to us. Selling the experience of a sailboat is an extremely different experience from selling the sailboat. Selling the sunsets and the wind in your face, along with the guarantee of training, product guarantees, and integrity (and a christening of the boat by the dealer, complete with champagne and a video) is what the customer desires. The sailboat is only the product. The extreme selling features and extreme service issues are what capture the heart of the consumer. We want them to fall in love with us (the experience) first and the product second.

No fine print or no guarantee

"Quality is not only right, it is free. And, it is not only free, it is the most profitable product line we have."

—Phil Crosby

When we use extreme customer service guarantees such as value-added warranties and guarantees, we need to create them in short form with no fine print. Otherwise, they're completely useless. If the fine print weakens the offer, you're better off not including it in your program.

Sadly, Americans expect a lack of quality. By and large they get what they expect. The reason is that procedure driven companies look at cost savings, not customer gaining. In 1990, the Malcolm Baldridge Award Winner was the Xerox Corporation's Business Products and Services Division. During the 1980s, Xerox felt its market share slipping away. In 1984, it began its quest for quality. The company identified four major core principles to help guide it to success.

The first and most important core principle is customer satisfaction (extreme customer service would dictate the word "satisfaction" be replaced with "delight"). The other three principles, of equal importance to one another are:

1. Achieving projected return on assets.
2. Increasing market share.
3. Maintaining a topflight work force.

Xerox went on to identify these core values:

- Achieve success by satisfying customers.
- Deliver quality and excellence in all things.
- Maintain a premium return on assets.
- Acquire superior technology to develop leadership in the marketplace.
- Develop employees to their fullest potential.
- Act as a responsible corporate citizen.

It should be of major significance that a global leader, a company that created the most powerful brand identity in business during three decades considered its most important growth strategy to be the satisfaction of its customers.

Total Quality Management discusses the powerful motivational payoffs that come from shifting the paradigm of monarchical behavior to one of democratic behavior. Let's review some of the issues that can relate to your organization. If you're a manager, owner, or employee:

Shift from:	To:
Firefighting.	Fire prevention.
Individual work.	Teamwork.
Command decisions.	Consensus decisions.
Focusing on the task.	Focusing on the customer.
Bosses and subordinates.	Everyone's an expert.
Control by fear.	Control through positive reinforcement.
One correct approach.	Creative solutions/improvement.
Disguised vision and values.	Shared vision and values.
Shoot from the hip.	Gather data first.
Blame/Cover your butt.	Problem solving.

Extreme customer service behavior begins at the beginning. Your number one priority is to outservice your competition. This chart that shifts you from old behavior to new behavior is helpful because it reinforces issues affecting your team. By now, we recognize that top-down management works because owners and managers are models within organizations. If we look back to the research, anti-hypocrisy is top-of-mind today. If you say something to an employee, be prepared to live it yourself.

Your organization is not a machine. Rather, it is a living and breathing entity that can and must change and grow. If your employees begin to feel that they don't work for the company, but that they are part of the company, then extreme customer service behavior will begin. Remember that there are costs and rewards to change. The costs are minor if the rewards of change are valuable to the organization.

Celebrate contributions

Aside from the standard rewards of salary increases and bonuses, rewards can come in other forms. For example, you can celebrate with trophies, T-shirts, motivational events (as we've discussed before), or personal letters from the company heads touting the wonderful contributions made by the employees. Herb Kelleher, a brilliantly creative extreme customer service contributor, stamps the back of each paycheck to the entire staff with the words: "From the customer." The employee who performs admirably already knows this, but it's something that each team member can benefit from.

The Japanese ask, "What can I do for the team?"; American businesses ask, "What can the team do for me?" There is a profound difference between the two. Extreme customer service states that the team is employee and customer driven. What, as a business owner, can I do for them? The American philosophy has been, "what has been done for the company?" The difference is in attitude and greed. Short-term greed leads to long-term need!

Does your company's literature talk about *you* or *the customer*? Customer service is not me-oriented, it's you-oriented with specific emphasis on customer issues, not egotistical organizational issues. The idea is to increase your corporate energy by inviting intimacy from the customer. You do this by first eliminating fear (providing credibility, guarantees, value-added issues, extremely friendly demeanor, and creative problem solving) and then by continually inviting the customer to your door with quality-service ideas and offers. You also invite intimacy from your employees by eliminating their fear of reprisal for thinking as individuals. If people can speak without the fear of repercussions, then ideas flow freely! Even if you don't implement an employee's idea, include it in discussions and acknowledge the effort, if not the innovation.

When the boss becomes the mentor

"Change your thoughts and you change the world."
—Norman Vincent Peale

When the boss moves from dictator to motivator, from figurehead to coach, the team's motivational spirit climbs. You'll see more pride in the work, more camaraderie, more professionalism, more love for the work, more self-respect, and by far, the most important change: more extreme customer service attitudes!

The more power and authority you give to the team, the more you get. If the boundaries are clear, creativity can reign, not ruin. TQM points out that owners should never delegate anything that they wouldn't be willing to do themselves. This leads to a very innovative idea for companies to grow creatively: rotate leadership. Remember when schools would have a "Principal Day," where a student took over the role of principal? Consider doing the same in your own organization. It's enormously fun, totally inclusive, empowering, and it fosters diversity.

Teams fail when there's a complete lack of direction. Team members need to bring their own ideas to the table within a given framework, and not completely reinvent the framework (unless you're on the verge of bankruptcy). Teams also fail when the workers are isolated from the customers...where they don't get to see how what they do affects the customers. They also fail when given unrealistic goals and deadlines. Remember, don't manage behavior, manage people and behavior will change.

The Shewart/Deming Cycle

The Shewart/Deming Cycle is designed to communicate a simple procedure that produces Total Customer Satisfaction. Of course, extreme customer satisfaction takes it even one step further:

- **Plan:** Spend the time planning your purpose, your approach to customer issues.
- **Do:** Carry out your plan and test it to ensure that it produces the desired effect.
- **Study:** What effect has your plan had on the bigger picture? Is it affecting bottom line profits, repeat customer visits, increased sales, higher transactions?
- **Act:** If the results indicate a direction or continuation of the plan, then move from small scale application to complete application. Begin to act on the success of the first three elements of the satisfaction cycle. Add the following to your plan.

Get your products recommended!

Imagine if you could become the J.D. Power & Associates of your industry. Imagine further that you're the Consumer's Union for drill bits. Or corned beef. Or insurance.

Imagine if you could write your review for the customer to consider. It's fantastic thinking about the options. And because we're such an insecure society, we usually rely upon reviews. They tell us what movies to see, what plays, what food to eat, where to be seen, what cars to buy, what detergent to use, and on and on. Imagine if you could create reviews and your salespeople could relate them based upon the experiences of both staff and customers alike. Sound silly? Not really.

J.D. Power & Associates was recently featured in *The New York Times Magazine,* where it was written that their rapid rise came from polling the public and ignoring the experts, threatening the elitism of traditional consumer research groups like Consumers Union. The *Times* asked the questions, "Whose opinion should matter?"

You could poll your customers, suppliers, and employees, creating product or service reviews that you could use to build confidence among your customers. This is a great tool for turning *prospects* into *customers* by relating what your present customers think about your company and its service.

Public opinion builds business

Companies actually pay J.D. Power to poll the public about their products in order to gain a competitive advantage. Confident companies roll the dice in order to gain this valuable assessment. Zagat does it in the food industry by polling diners about specific restaurants, writing reviews that the public uses as a guide in choosing a place to eat. After all, who's more credible, the consuming public or some ivory tower critic?

Remember the "Good Housekeeping Seal of Approval"? Today, it's the J.D. Power Seal of Approval. According to a 1999 Harris poll commissioned by the firm, 63 percent of American adults have heard of J.D. Power—up from 55 percent from three years ago. What this tells us is that customers would like to know what other customers think. It helps in the decision-making process and it helps enormously in the issue of customer service.

Basically, J.D. Power advises companies on how to improve "customer satisfaction." The company sends a questionnaire that includes a one-dollar incentive for a response. As the *Times* article explained, "The surveys fall into two broad categories: "proprietary studies," commissioned by individual companies seeking objective information about their own customers' needs and desires; and "syndicated studies" that rank competing products or services within a particular industry based on customer satisfaction."

The rankings were used to successfully tout the achievements of the companies. The top performers then receive awards that are used in advertising. The company points out that it isn't really J.D. Power that is awarding the company, it's the public. Think about it...what if your company were to publish, promote, create signage, direct mail, or scripts for salespeople that communicated poll results from existing customers? What if you did it on an ongoing basis?

What if your poll reflected both product and service issues that you could then use to sell and use as a barometer for maintaining high product/service integrity and extreme customer service behavior? It might change the face of your organization and keep your team members continually and obsessively interested in their performance. When the customer is permitted to review the company, the company then uses those reviews to invite new customers in. This is a magical combination that promotes both product satisfaction and customer excitement.

For example, Zagat published a review of "Le Cirque" that is glowing—from food to service. The review is based upon customers who have eaten there, who are writing the review for other customers. The Gallup organization does the same thing for public opinion about politics and social issues. Consumer Reports uses their team of experts instead of the customer and their rankings are sometimes vastly different from the public opinion polls. The goal of J.D. Power & Associates is to make businesses recognize their self-interest in giving customers what they want. Give your customers what they want by polling them about both product and service—then use the results to promote specific products. What if 63 percent of your customers responded that they have never gotten the kind of extreme customer service that you offer?

A true or false quality quiz

To round up this chapter, here is a simple test to see how well you've retained many of the ideas presented here. Answer each question true or false:

1. Higher quality leads to lower productivity? ______________
2. Since the customer (not the organization) defines quality, the customer is always right? ______________
3. "Doing it right the first time" is a Total Quality Management philosophy? ______________
4. Inspecting quality (for example, a customer service transaction) at the end of a task is the only true way of guaranteeing quality? ______________
5. When the customer is completely satisfied, then the quality-driven organization has done its job? ______________
6. Effectively "putting out fires" in an organization is a valid method of achieving customer satisfaction? ______________

Here are the answers:

1. *False.* Higher quality does not lead to lower productivity. It's quite the opposite. Higher quality does not mean that more time must be spent on production of products or carrying out services...it actually increases the productivity by ensuring fewer returns, customer service issues, and employee frustration.
2. *False.* The customer is always the customer. The customer does define quality, product, and service to a large degree. But since "right" and "wrong" are indefinable terms, the concept is that the customer is always responsible for the ongoing success of the business. As such, the customer needs come first.
3. *True.* "Doing it right the first time" is critical. It increases productivity, lowers customer complaints, and increases employee morale.
4. *False.* Quality guarantees come before and after the task is completed. The quality experience begins in the selling process and continues throughout the relationship. Once the task is completed, the issue of quality can be assessed, but it clearly is not the only way of guaranteeing quality.

5. *False.* When customers are merely satisfied, they look elsewhere. When they are excited and delighted, they send others to you. Exceed their needs and you've achieved the goals of a quality-driven organization.
6. *False.* Elimination of the source of fires is a critical issue. By anticipating flare-ups and altering the course, a company achieves a much greater balance and spends less time cleaning up after its own mess.

Chapter 11

Be Outrageous...As Long As You Create the Right Rage

Forbes magazine ran a cover story listing America's top salespeople. Included in the list were Arnold Schwarzenegger, Michael Jordan, Ralph Lauren, and Sid Friedman. Who's Sid? He's an insurance salesman who, though he supervises thirty salespeople still works a full day selling himself. Sid's statement relates to his philosophy of serving customers. According to Murray Raphel and Neil Raphel, authors of *Up the Loyalty Ladder*, Sid's attitude was, "if it ain't broke, break it!" It's not enough simply to do what everyone else is doing. And, more importantly, it is not enough simply to repeat that which worked before. Peter Drucker writes that "every business has to be prepared to change everything!"

Sid says that simply because an idea or concept worked for years doesn't mean that it will continue to work for years. Sid believes in a very personal approach to staying in touch with both prospects and customers. It's the way he works and lives. And, in the insurance business, selling yourself is essential. There is no such thing as inaccessibility when it comes to customers. My clients have my cellular phone number, my beeper number, and the number for my private line at home. The commitment I make is to always be available.

Sid told me a story which has actually happened to many friends of mine in different industries. A client of his could not keep an appointment with because he was going to Chicago. So, Sid asked what time he was leaving in the morning. The client said that he was on the 7 a.m. flight. He then asked the client if he was flying first class or coach—the client was flying first class. Sid then asked if he could join him for the two-hour flight in order to conduct their business. The client said, "Absolutely! Come on board!"

Sid called the airline, got a ticket seated next to his client, and did a two-hour presentation. He walked away with a sale and flew home.

A story in *Reader's Digest* told of an example of service by a North Carolina police officer. While waiting for his son to arrive at Charlotte Douglas International Airport, Larry Rouse of Charlotte, North Carolina, sat in his car at a "no parking" zone. When his son didn't arrive, Larry left the car and went inside to check the flight schedule. When he returned, he discovered a ticket on his windshield. He realized at that point that he'd left his car keys in the terminal so he went back in to retrieve them.

When he returned, he found a second ticket on his windshield, whereupon he summoned the officer and explained that he deserved the first ticket but not the second. The officer understood the problem and took back the ticket. Larry also explained the situation regarding his son. As Larry was about to drive away, the officer approached again, much to Larry's chagrin. "You know," said the officer, "I appreciate the way you spoke to me. Most people aren't quite so kind. Let me tear up the first ticket, too. And have a good day."

In *Tales of Knock Your Socks Off Service*, Kristin Anderson and Ron Zemke gathered stories of various degrees of service to customers. The story of Alan Wilk, a man with a passion for clogged drains and a passion for customers, is one worth noting.

Wilk is a Roto Rooter employee with a penchant for cleaning the most stubborn of drains and sewers in New York City; a man Schlesinger calls, "a one-man rescue squad." Schlesinger profiled Wilk with the heading, "There are a million clogged drains in the Naked City, and one man can clean them all."

It seems that Wilk showed up at the house of a man named Charlie Mihulka over in Queens, New York, one night. The pipe connecting the house to the main sewer was clogged and four sewer and drain companies had already failed to clear it. It appeared that they had no other choice but through expensive options, such as a very expensive high-pressure jet truck or completely digging up and replacing the pipe. Apparently, this was the type of situation Wilk relished. Wilk attacked the problem as only an obsessive pipe cleaner would. He discovered that the pipe had a deep sag in it. The ground had settled beneath the pipe, bending it into a V as it carried its cargo from the house in the sewer main. Alan described the sludge as having the consistency of oatmeal mixed with tar. The sludge was blocking the pipe, but all of Wilk's efforts with the snake only cut into the sludge rather than clearing it.

Alan sat down and began to plan. "Technique sometimes gets you further than brute strength." he thought. Alan decided on a wire-brush disk which he fastened to the end of his snake. The spinning disk would attack the sludge while Alan pumped water into the pipe to keep the sludge flowing in the right direction. It worked and the pipe cleared. After all was finished, Alan saved the customer between $600 (the amount for the jet truck) and $2,000 (the amount for a new pipe). Charlie Milhulka got Wilk for less than a hundred. Alan's commitment to the customer reaches way beyond cost savings. It involves his attitude of concern and commitment and his absolute love of what he does.

What's the bottom line to Alan's extreme approach to problem solving? Most years, he's the among the highest producers in the company, often earning in excess of $70,000. At 50 years old, Alan Wilk has achieved a sense of purpose within Roto Rooter that has left his peers envious...and his customers truly appreciative.

Another story from Anderson and Zemke's contributors is about the National Park Service going above and beyond the call of duty. Jim Dehlman, a New York visitor to a historic site in Georgia, found an unusual helping of Southern hospitality. Dehlman flew to Atlanta for a visit with his brother. The two had scheduled a drive south of the city to visit the historic site at Andersonville, an old Civil War stockade and cemetery.

One of the brothers had car trouble and didn't arrive at the site until 5:25 p.m. only to discover that the park closed at 5:30 p.m. Dehlman noticed someone coming out of the administration building and drove to the entrance area. The gate was still partially open, so he walked up and knocked on the door.

Ranger Marsh answered and listened to the story regarding the brothers' meeting and the fact that they would not be able to see the sight due to their schedules. Ranger Alan Marsh opened the park, offered them a pontoon boat to tour the area, and told them to take their time in doing so. Says Dehlman, "When we finished, he met up with us again, told us a little more about Andersonville, answered all of our questions, and then showed us the graves of the six renegades that we had been unable to find. All of this after closing hours, on what I'm sure was his own time. All in all, the courtesy, hospitality, and compassion he showed us was amazing." Ranger Alan Marsh broke the rules to service the customer. He did so with passion, concern, caring, and friendship.

Making promises you *almost* can keep

Back when James Barksdale was COO of Federal Express, he apologized to a group of executives at a quality conference. His apology related to the fact that in reality only 98 percent of Federal Express packages arrived on time. That meant that, with over 800,000 packages and letters, 2 percent translated to 16,000 packages that arrived later than promised. He apologized because he said that he could certainly not brag too loudly about 16,000 packages that had gone astray.

Companies that achieve excellence in service stand out. Their character includes the fact that the owners and managers have tunnel vision when it comes to the customer. They are hands-on in dealing with customers, living, eating, and breathing service in their day-to-day business lives. Every system—from the order taking to the checkout and the payment programs—every system is customer-service friendly. They balance high-tech with high-touch...including a personal touch with every bit of technological advancement. They audition and carefully qualify candidates based on attitude toward customers and psychological profiles. They market both internally to the employees and externally to their customers so that everyone is on the same page. They also constantly measure the benefits of the service and share successes with employees.

Over 88 percent of the American work force are involved in service jobs. Think about services that affect your own life: dry cleaning, hair cuts, TV repairs, automobile repairs, plumbers, electricians, painters, eyeglasses, hearing aids, the florist, pizza delivery...the list is endless. Because mediocrity reigns, outrageous service stories are still an anomaly. Innovative services include such things as computer dating, fast food delivery, kids' shops, software search firms, shopping services, massages at your home, house and pet sitting services...all of the ideas that stem from people thinking about what other people really want, need, and will appreciate.

12 outrageous service philosophies

Remember Sid Friedman? He lists 12 secrets of outrageous customer-service philosophies. Let's take a look at them and look at ways to possibly make them even more outrageous.

1. Promise a lot and deliver even more. Overstate and overservice your customer. Simply outpromise the competition and deliver more than you promised. If the customer wants it Tuesday, promise it, then call to let them know it's ready Monday.
2. One hundred percent is a good starting point. If we had to live with only 99.9 percent, we'd have one hour of unsafe drinking water every month, two unsafe plane landings at Chicago's O'Hare Airport every day, 16,000 pieces of mail lost every hour, and 500 incorrect surgical performances every week.
3. Be the consummate expert. An expert knows what he or she is doing every time. An expert stays abreast of changes and incorporates them into his or her information bank. An expert analyzes self-performance, looking for ways toward enhancing him- or herself.
4. Keep a creative notebook. If you hear or read something innovative, write it down and incorporate it into your own business agenda.
5. Maintain excitement in the journey and dream about the destination.
6. Envision the growth of your business through acts of uncompromised kindness toward customers. Then imagine the benefits of being number one in your market and capturing mindshare!

7. Create a "personal best" program that details the demonstrative actions you will take every day to create new selling opportunities and new loyal customers.
8. Segregate tasks into "urgent," "important," and "everything else." Then, recognize that your number one urgent priority is to develop ownership of just 10 new customers per month.
9. Incorporate the four Ds of time control: do it, delay it, delegate it, or destroy it.
10. Look at the competition and think in opposites. In other words, stop competing and start creating. Value-added service is one great way to create rather than compete.
11. Get a coach if you're not an incredibly positive person. If you're the owner or manager, let a professional acting coach help you create a business persona. It will grow your business and make your life better too.
12. Eliminate losers and losing philosophies from your business. Don't you ever let them come in contact with your customers.

Sometimes simple is the smartest way to go

If you attend seminars on marketing and customer service, you've noticed that outrageous gestures need not be limited to before the sale...and, in fact, after the sale customer service is serious business and a smart way to up repeat sales. The Gap, Nordstrom, Radio Shack, *The New Yorker* Magazine, Pier 1, and many other companies have incredible programs for after-the-sale service.

The letter you send after the sale not only thanks the customer, it *really* thanks them. It offers the customer a sense of their importance to the company. However, when customers get amazing home-baked cookies for a simple $50 purchase, it's outrageous to them. Or, how about the steak dinner a printer sent to me for simply inquiring about an estimate for a large color printing job? Outrageous and extreme service? You bet it is.

Just do it!

Hal Becker, author of *At Your Service*, decided to write to 10 companies that were doing outrageous things to gain and hold onto business. He called each one and asked them questions about their philosophy and practices in regard to customer service. First, he noted that in almost every case, each company hired "positive energy thinkers." The critical factor for every company is not a skill, background, or educational degree, but an aspect of personality that reflects their ideal behavior.

The second area he noted was the absence of rules. Not one single company had a 100-page policy manual dictating everything from company hours to appropriate dress. Instead, each company had ongoing training to educate their people on how to take care of the problems they might encounter in business. I'd like to relate a few of the stories that illustrate our premise.

Let's look at Callaway, a golf club company with a reputation for excellence and innovation. Hal Becker's mother is a golfer who owned Callaway's infamous "Big Bertha" golf club. The shaft on the club broke and she returned it to the retailer where she had purchased it. The shop owner, an obvious member of our club of losers, gave her nothing but unsatisfactory run-arounds without solving any of her problems. Frustrated, she called Callaway and asked for customer service. They listened. Then they decided to quickly solve her problem by asking her to return the broken club by mail (they would pick up the cost) and they would rush her a new club immediately. They also explained that they had little control over the behavior of their retailers. Outrageous? No...but certainly adequate. Outrageous or extreme service would have included a dozen free golf balls for her troubles. Outrageous behavior exceeds the need and goes at least one step further than fixing the problem...it over-fixes in order to delight rather than satisfy. Becker's mother was satisfied and got what she should have from the get-go. Extreme customer service takes it one step further and creates complete ownership of the customer.

Look at L.L Bean. Founded in 1912 by Leon Leonwood Bean, the company opened its first retail store in 1917 in Freeport, Maine. That store remains open 24 hours a day, 365 days per year, and draws more than 3.5 million "guests" each year. Outrageous? I'd say so. How do they do it? Extreme customer service! Their customer satisfaction department (I wish they'd change it to "customer delight department") also operates 24 hours a day, each and every day of the year. The company receives 14 million toll-free catalog and customer service calls each year. Telephone orders account for 80 percent of all orders with mail orders accounting for the other 20 percent. The philosophy about customer service has changed somewhat over the years. It used to be that the company treated the customer the way the company wanted to be treated. Now, they say that they want to treat the customer the way the customer wants to be treated. There's a difference. Further, they train customer service people that they are not employed to match wits with the customer. The customer may have a situation where they can be helped with information, but they will get whatever they ask for that's reasonable and right.

When asked what makes them the best in their type of business, they immediately reply: customer service. They have a 100-percent guarantee for the life of the product and they are renowned for a phone "attitude" that is helpful, polite, and endearing.

"We only have one rule: Use good judgment in all situations!"

Earlier on, I told you how impressed I was with the Ritz Carlton Hotel chain and their ingenious mission statement: "Ladies and gentlemen serving ladies and gentlemen." This chain is not a franchise, like many other hotels, but rather they are owned by a management company. What makes them so special is their service. This begins with management's insistence that every employee carry a "credo card" with the quote above printed on it. It serves as a reminder that the Ritz Carlton experience is about sophisticated service with an emphasis on "anything we can do to please." What makes the credo so interesting is that, in bottom-line terms, it communicates that if you want to be treated like a gentleman, you must act like a gentleman. If you want to be treated like a doorman, act like a doorman. It's brilliant, because it empowers the employees to understand the guest better. According to Hal Becker, Ritz Carlton has 20 basics that are part of its program of customer service. Outrageous? You decide!

Becker points out that the employee entrance to some of the Ritz Carlton hotels has these 20 basics hanging from blue signs. They're also printed on little plastic cards in order to reinforce their importance. Some of these rules are printed here for your benefit. For example, number eight is: "Any employee who receives a customer complaint owns the complaint." The first level employees (housekeepers and busboys) can spend up to $2,000 of the hotel's money at any time to satisfy a customer's needs. Managers have the authority to spend $5,000. Is that outrageous enough for you?

Number nine is pretty good too. "To pacify the customer instantly...and follow up within 20 minutes in order to ensure that the problem has been solved." Number 12 states: "To smile, always be on stage, and maintain positive eye contact." Number 14 is wonderful as well: "To escort guests, rather than pointing out directions." Remember Nordstrom's philosophy of having each salesperson leave the counter, walk around it, hand the customer the purchase and shake hands? It's the same here.

Ninety-six percent of Ritz Carlton's employees said that "excellence in guest services" was a top priority, even though 3,000 of those employees have been with the hotel for less than three years. Pride is rampant at Ritz Carlton. Employees truly feel and act like ambassadors for the company and are given a level of authority that is unsurpassed in the hospitality industry. Outrageous? There's no question in my mind!

Extreme customer service relies upon competition and repetition

Charles Schwab spends a great deal of money advertising, and they create an extreme customer service selling proposition based upon researching the competition, finding voids, and filling them. A recent *New York Times Magazine* full-page advertisement read: "Susan doesn't worry about Schwab's investment specialists' being in it for the commission...they don't get one." The ad is accompanied by a photo of their ideal customer, an attractive working mother who says, "At Schwab, they put me first."

This example shows the connection they make between greed, economies, and the rest of the customer service story—which includes "no sales pressure," empathetic investment specialists, responsiveness, and reiteration of the fact that the salespeople are salaried.

When we recognize excellence in the companies out there, we need to reward them. We need to encourage them to continue to treat us magnificently by becoming loyal to these companies. It's a wonderful way to fight the indifference that runs rampant in airlines, banking, food service, automobile retailing, insurance, and so forth. The fact is that companies who live by the credo, "The more you do for people, the more people come to you," are companies who recognize that they are in business to make people happy...not to sell products or services. If they make people happy, people buy their products and services.

One of my all-time favorite actors, Jimmy Stewart, once said, "I never think of my audiences as customers, I think of them as partners." If we think of our customers as partners, we realize that they are indeed our partners in the success of the business. They are sharing the experience as well as creating revenue for us. It's an interesting twist.

The soothing sounds of Southwest

We couldn't possibly discuss outrageous customer service without including Southwest Airlines. There is no company I've ever heard of that includes *fun* as one of its principle objectives—and accomplishes it. Southwest Airlines has shown a profit for the past quarter of a century...each and every year. Hal Becker calls the airline "my absolute favorite company of all." I can see why.

Even though Southwest has no first class section on its planes, no assigned seating, sophisticated food service, special baggage handling, or any other amenities whatsoever, they continually exceed customer expectations. This has to do with Southwest's safety record, on-time service, and amazing attitude toward the customer.

Herb Kelleher, president, hires people based on a three-point "must-have" system. First, each candidate must possess extraordinary enthusiasm. Next, a keen sense of humor. Finally, an outstanding attitude. Frequent flyers are actually asked to help hire other employees for the airline. According to Herb, customers know what they want and don't want in service. Employees are encouraged to break the rules in the interest of customer service, and Herb is said to know almost all 14,000 people in his organization by first name. He never says "I" but instead gives credit to everybody else. Employee turnover is six percent—one of the lowest you'll find. Another amazing fact about Southwest is that employees hire employees and all people in the company cross-train one another, which means you may see a vice president working at the gate to understand each aspect of the business. Pilots hire pilots, so they're accountable for their choices. Southwest describes its philosophies of doing business as "crazy like a fox."

Hal Becker observed some of the more outrageous examples of good humor. For instance, at the ticket counter, you might be asked to remove your shoes in order to see how many holes you have in your socks. The person with the most holes gets a drink coupon for the flight. You might also be asked to take out your wallet and count your credit cards. The person with the most cards gets a free drink as well. The company is so irreverent and outrageous that Herb is purported to run through the offices in different costumes to "shake things up a bit."

When you're on the plane, you may hear the pilot say: "Hello, this is the pilot of flight number 121. We have a little problem, but please don't be concerned, it's nothing to worry about. You see, our automatic bag smasher is broken so we're smashing all the bags by hand. Please be patient." People's anxiety goes away and their laughter abounds. Most people can't believe that they're allowed to have fun and that the airline is allowed to make them laugh. After all, what's so serious about flying? It's supposed to be fun, isn't it?

One of the greatest stories about the airline involves a man who is running to the gate, angry and late. There's one seat left on the plane. Unbeknownst to the passenger, there is a small flight attendant stuffed into the overhead baggage compartment. The passenger is sweaty, tired, and huffing and puffing. He gets to the only seat left and pops open the compartment. The entire plane is in on the joke and can't wait for his reaction. The little flight attendant jumps up in the compartment and asks the passenger, "May I take this for you, sir?"

What's the deal? Well, to begin with the mission and vision of the company is to sell an experience that comforts, nurtures, humors, and offers friendship and fun. The company has a spirit that is really unequalled because of the unique vision of its leader—a self-effacing jokester who knows how to make people feel comfortable. Creativity and care for customers and employees alike is what makes the company special, which translates right to the bottom line in profits and repeat business.

Sometimes he wins, sometimes he loses, but he's always making waves

"Expose yourself to the best things humans have done and then try to bring those things into what you are doing."
— Steve Jobs, Apple/NeXT/Pixar

Like him or hate him, Steve Jobs has changed the face of technology. In his "insanely" outrageous book, *The Circle of Innovation*, Tom Peters notes how Jobs believes that every product or any product can be insanely great...but the first requirement in making the product great is great people. For his product development teams, Jobs hires individuals with "intriguing backgrounds" and "extraordinary taste." For example, he's been known to hire poets and historians, in addition to techies. Their magic, according to Jobs, is that, "...they have exposed themselves to the best things humans have done and then brought those things into their projects." The original Macintosh team was a melange of artists and engineers. They owned "user-friendly" as a concept because half the team was made up of nontechies. Peters challenges us by asking, "Have you hired any poets, artists, or historians lately? I'm serious."

In *The Drama of Leadership*, Patricia Pitcher states, "You say you don't want emotional, volatile, and unpredictable—just imaginative? Sorry, they only come in a package...I can offer you a dedicated, loyal, honest, realistic, knowledgeable package, but the imagination bit will be rather limited."

When you look to your own people, empower them with the kind of authority we've discussed here. When you encourage them to recognize that business and fun can be synonymous, you're beginning to expand your horizons. So, when a company does something as simple as a silly gesture to create some laughter, we recognize just how outrageous that simple gesture is in the skies of mediocrity and mundane behavior.

Becoming outrageous, audacious, and irreverent is not easy for those who haven't exercised their creativity for some time. But, it's worth the trip and extreme customer service behavior begins by looking at your organization and thinking about removing all the rules and replacing them with chaos and anarchy. Just for a moment, think about what it would be like if you told your people they could do anything for the customer that was not immoral, illegal, unethical, or blatantly unprofitable in the long run?

Chapter 12

Civility and Business... Mutually Exclusive?

"Nice people are always at the mercy of people who are not nice."
—Samuel Nulman, humanitarian

When I was growing up, my father would never, ever honk the car horn when we were picking up a friend at their home. He would simply gesture for me to get out of the car, ring the bell, and let my friend know we were there. Though he could have afforded a luxury car, he drove Oldsmobiles because, as he put it, "my friends can't afford Cadillacs." He was a man of unusual civility and intellect, a man who truly believed in the consideration of others—in business and in life.

Civility sometimes seems like a foreign concept in business today. Technology companies are fighting traditional businesses, service quality is at an all-time low, recruitment competition is so keen that "signing bonuses" are the norm in many industries. Nurses today can name their price within a huge range...and demand a bonus for committing to one particular organization. It's an amazing time.

Kindness is clearly at the heart of what I call extreme customer service behavior. Common sense is rampant throughout everything we've discussed. The idea of being kind and considerate to the customer shouldn't be worthy of one book—much less a multitude of books. It should simply be a given. The fact that simple civility is so hard to find creates enormous opportunity for the entrepreneurial business owner. It's just a question of deciding who you want to be tomorrow.

Courting the customer

Seduction. Romance. Engagement. Marriage. They're the four stages of a relationship in life, as well as in business. We are, after all, emotional creatures who respond to touch, feelings, warmth, cold, intellectual stimulation—and all of these elements go into building a relationship. The truth is that when we court a customer, we're telling them that we want them in a relationship with us. It's really as simple as that. Even angry customers can be courted. You know the types: easily frustrated, penny-wise and pound-foolish, quick to anger, frantic, unfriendly, and uncaring. The best way to "disarm" these types of people is to agree with them. Pure and simple. By agreeing with a customer you immediately become an ally instead of an adversary. Once you're an ally, the customer's defenses drop and communication opens up. Disarmament in extreme customer service is a tactic that takes place passively. In war, it occurs as a result of aggression.

Customers are always right if you make them right

"Never argue with people when they're right."
— Samuel Nulman

When I was a teenager, I worked in a pharmacy as a delivery driver and store clerk. About twice a week, an elderly man with a scraggly face and bent body came in for his gum and other incidentals. Every time he arrived, the dialogue was exactly the same.

I knew he had only little money because of his appearance, the way he addressed me, and the way he counted out his change. And I knew he loved Wrigley's Spearmint Gum.

The typical exchange went something like this: "Mr. Koransky, how are you today?" I would say. He would reply, "Ain't worth a damn, don't give a damn!"

This script played out each and every time I saw him. He made his purchase, struggled to count the change, and left. I inquired about him and my boss explained that he was just a tired, old, lonely guy who lost his wife years ago and had nothing to do but walk around the neighborhood. He spent a great deal of his time sitting on a park bench in the little park adjacent to the pharmacy.

One day I noticed that he tore a stick of gum into three pieces, rewrapping the pieces and stuffing them back into the pack. Clearly he was hoarding the gum to save money and make each package last longer. I asked the boss if I could purchase a retail case of 24 packages of the gum and he sold it to me at cost. When Mr. Koransky arrived the next time, I handed him the case of gum in a brown bag and told him it was a gift for his loyalty to the store. He did something I couldn't quite believe. A slight smile wrinkled his face and he looked as though tears were filling his eyes. He said, "Thank you son...but now I've got no reason to come in to the store." Before he could turn and leave, I told him that he didn't need to make a purchase in order to stop in and say hello...in fact I was sure that if he stopped coming everyone who worked in the pharmacy would miss him. He stood there and stared directly into my eyes...his head nodding slightly as he spoke. "Young man, thank you for being kind to a worthless old man." He turned and left. Each time thereafter (until he ran out of gum) he would come in and say hello, look around for a few minutes and walk out.

Talk to your customers and see if they talk back

"Friendship is the inexpressible comfort of having to neither weigh thoughts nor measure words."
—Anonymous

A medical center near my office used to have a policy (that is, until they got bigger) that included a follow-up phone call after a visit. When I had strep throat some years ago, the next day someone called to see how I was feeling. It made me feel good and it made me loyal.

Each occasion you have to communicate with the customer is another building block in the relationship...even if you have little or no reason to call. Customers want to do business with people who care...and when you call just to see how they're doing, they feel cared for. Remember this is not a sales call, it's a call to build a relationship.

When I worked in the pharmacy, I was never trained in customer service...the owners didn't seem to care. But, I was trained in civility by my father, who taught me to help people. So, when a customer was looking for a particular shampoo, I never pointed my finger in a direction...I came out from behind the counter and found the product for the customer.

Your future in business depends upon your treatment of the customer. Bill Gates, in his book *The Road Ahead*, explores how the Internet will change things forever. Customers are going to the Net in order to access all the information they need to make an intelligent buying decision. They'll find the best price, features, benefits, and delivery. The only thing they can't get is an interpersonal relationship...at least not yet. This revolution in selling products and services can only be effectively countered by extreme customer service. Sure, your customers will be better informed and better ready to use this information to get what they want from you...but what they really want in addition to the features mentioned above is *you*. People, for the most part, want to do business with people...but only if they're exceptional people. Otherwise they'll be just as happy to go to the Internet where they get everything else.

What's your story?

Remember that most huge businesses began as small businesses with big ideas and big service stories. OfficeMax started with one store in Mayfield Heights, Ohio...but they had a big idea and a big service story. In your own business, what drives you to please the customer? Is it passion, money, wanting to beat the competition, a personal goal to please, your sincere desire to be nice, a keen sense of civility—or is it a combination of many of these and other factors? Civility begins by simply saying *yes* to the customer, and, by recognizing that the customer is your most valued asset...more than inventory, technology, systems, operations, trucks, parts, buildings...all of which would collapse without an ongoing extreme commitment to the customer.

So, what's your story?

- Do you finish stocking a shelf when a customer's waiting?
- Do you keep a customer anxious while you stare at the computer screen in order to check on the rental car?
- Do you continue to wipe the counter when a customer is waiting to pay for his coffee?
- Do you consult the "manager" before deciding to please a customer?
- Do you play music in your place of business that might distract the customer or disturb his or her sensibilities?
- Do you simply say, "Have a nice day," when you should be saying, "I greatly appreciate your business and look forward to serving you again soon."
- Do you sell the product instead of selling the customer?
- Do you ask for three forms of identification before cashing a recognized customer's check?
- Do you offer a three-percent introductory rate with fine print which indicates that the rate will jump in two months?
- Do you pressure the customer in order to fulfill a quota?
- Do you sell the customer products or services they don't need in order to win a sales contest?
- Do you carelessly toss the customer's baggage onto the plane?
- Do you look annoyed when the customer takes time to make a decision?
- Do you entice customers by indicating that if they buy immediately they'll save substantially?
- Do you con the customer in any way, shape, or form?
- Do you attempt to get the customer to buy additional insurance they don't need when renting your product?
- Do you tell your customer that a reasonable request is difficult or impossible?
- Do you put the customer on edge by indicating that all sales are final?
- Do you treat the customer with committed concern and care or with **indifference**?

It's your business and it's your future. Extreme customer service begins by recognizing what is easily recognized...the customers's feelings. You are selling an individual, not a commodity, and you are serving people, not gross margins. It's easy to be nice if you understand that it will not only make you feel much better about yourself...it'll make the customer feel much better about you!

Index

A

A.C. Neilsen, 83, 125-126
Airlines
  examples of good service on, 178-180
  problems with, 31-35, 93-95, 100
Allstate, 24
American Society for Quality Service, 10-11, 34, 135
Anderson, Kristin, 62, 64, 170-171
Apple, 62, 180
Arc of Triumph, 93-94
Attachment, 98, 101, 107

B

Baby boomers, 144-148
Banks
  positive examples of, 62-63
  problems with, 45-46
  reinventing, 46, 62-63
Brand(s),
  as megatrend, 139-140
  of low-priced commodities, 113-114
  smaller as better, 65-66
Buying cycle, 97-99

C

Circle of Innovation, 41, 65
Civility, 23-24, 71-92, 181-186
  examples of, 73-75, 77, 106-107, 182-184
Common sense, 71-92
Competitors, 43-44, 46, 177-178
Conditioned responses, 11
Convenience, 22-23
Customer Intimacy, 56-57, 61, 115
Customer Loyalty, 36, 47, 96
Customer(s)
  abusing policies, 67-68, 77-78
  as friends, 37-39, 47-48

as salespeople, 40-41
dangers in stereotyping, 131-133
fighting for rights as, 79-81, 100
ID, 156-157
love from, 36-37, 96, 104-105, 124-126, 140
"owning," 12, 31-32, 46-47, 52-53
public opinion, 164-165
"romancing," 37-39, 62
treating as celebrities, 20-22, 88-89, 131-133
why they buy, 97-100
win/win situations, 99
worth of, 46-47, 128-129
Customizing, 17-19, 106

D

Databases, 49-57
Dave's Bagels, 89-92
Diamond of Loyalty, 124-125
Disney, 99-100

E

e-businesses, 23
Employees
creating passion in, 74
dangers of retaining erring, 83-84, 157-158
encouraging change, 153-154, 158-159
following company's purpose, 152-156
keeping motivated, 44-45, 85-86, 161-163
knowing purpose of company, 151-152
training, 80-82, 87, 130-131
types of, 130-131
Experience, 13-14, 39-40, 138

F

Fear
in buying, 23-24
overcoming, 23-26, 36-37
Ford, 47
Fun, 74, 88, 107-108
Futurists, 135-149

G

Gallup, 11-12
Garmany, 49
Girard, Joe, 47-48
Griffin, Jill, 36, 47, 96-98

H

Harley Davidson, 37-38

I

IBM, 61-62
Ignorance, 13
Incentives, 44-45
Indifference, 83, 89, 100-101
Infiniti, 50-51
Internet, 23, 77-78,

J

J.D. Power & Associates, 163-166
Jobs, Steve, 62, 180
Just saying yes, 10, 20, 131

K

Keeping Customers for Life, 13, 33, 35-37

Kelleher, Herb, 178-179
Koob-Cannie, Joan, 13, 33, 35-37

L

L.L. Bean, 67
Loyalty
    building, 39-41
    management, 98-99, 124-125
    schemes, 125-127

M

Megatrends, 136-143
Nine-point solution, 116-121

N

No problem, 10, 18, 79
Nordstrom, 10, 25, 41, 79, 111, 116

O

Outback, 26-27

P

Personality
    examples of, 75-76
    in creating passion, 74-75
    in the sale, 120-121
Peters, Tom, 41, 71, 74
Positioning, 14, 52-55
Price
    as secondary to service, 111
    vs. value, 121

Q

Quality quiz, 166-167
Quick Chek Food Stores, 34-35, 56, 82

R

Reynolds, Jim, 102-103
Ricardi, Gary, 146-149
Ritz Carlton, 51-52, 176-177
Rules, 76-78

S

Saturn, 40
Service
    boorish, 19-20, 73-74
    customer-driven, 13-14, 62, 104, 129
    extreme service checklist, 101
    risk reducing in, 14-16, 114-116
    selling as product, 108-110, 117, 119, 159-161, 172-173
    thanks through give-aways, 26-29, 174-176
    training to love customers, 130-131
    twelve outrageous service philosophies, 173-174
Shewart/Deming Cycle, 163
Size
    drawbacks to, 59-61
    in marketing, 59-69
SMART, 103-104, 155-156
Southwest Airlines, 178-180
Sprechler, Jay, 31
Surveys
    disadvantages of, 53
    sample of, 54
    using to discover company's niche, 57
    using to "hire" customers, 52-53
    using to identify needs, 53-55

T

Tales of Knock Your Socks Off Service, 62, 170
Team recognition, 11-12, 104-105
Triangle of Quality, 36

U

Upside-Down Flow Chart, 34

V

Voice mail, 127-128

W

Wacker, Watts, 135
Watson, Thomas, 61
What's in it for me?, 77-79
When America Does It Right, 31
Wiersema, Fred, 56, 61, 115

Z

Zemke, Ron, 62, 64, 171